WE MEET AGAIN

Praise for the series

TIMMY FAILURE

WE MEET AGAIN

Stephan Pastis

WALKER
BOOKS

First published in Great Britain 2014 by Walker Books Ltd
87 Vauxhall Walk, London SE11 5HJ

This edition published 2019

2 4 6 8 10 9 7 5 3 1

© 2014 Stephan Pastis
Timmy Failure font © 2012 Stephan Pastis

The right of Stephan Pastis to be identified as author of this
work has been asserted by him in accordance with the
Copyright, Designs and Patents Act 1988

This book has been typeset in Nimrod

Printed and bound by CPI Group (UK) Ltd, Croydon CR0 4YY

British Library Cataloguing in Publication Data:
a catalogue record for this book is available from the British Library

ISBN 978-1-4063-8672-1

www.walker.co.uk

www.timmyfailure.com

MIX
Paper from
responsible sources
FSC® C020471

A Prologue That Puts Me Between a Dog and a Hard Face and Lets You Guess Which One I'll Choose

The scariest thing you'll ever see is the thing you never see.

And such is the Scrum Bolo Chihuahua.

The Scrum Bolo Chihuahua is a gigantic four-ton Chihuahua who lives at the top of a grove of coastal redwood trees.

Best guess as to what it might look like

There, shrouded in fog, he listens for children.

And when he hears one, he leaps from the tree and steers his way down to the forest floor, using his giant Chihuahua ears.

And swallows the child whole.

Which is how he got so big.

BEFORE
EATING
CHILDREN

AFTER
EATING
CHILDREN

But the Scrum Bolo Chihuahua will not eat just *any* child.

The child must first be a camper at Camp Monkeychuck, a run-down cluster of cabins at the edge of the redwood grove.

Which is why the leaders of Camp Monkeychuck issue this warning to each and every new camper:

NEVER go into the redwood grove.

Which is why I am now in the redwood grove.

I am here because I am a world-class detective.

And the rules don't apply to us.

And so I wandered.

And I was brave.

But redwood trees can grow quickly. And soon new trees began to sprout all around me. And my once-clear path became filled with towering redwoods that were not there before.

And so I sat on the forest floor.

And watched as the ocean fog crept in around the trees.

And heard, above the thick mist, a faint sound.

"Arf, arf, arf, arf."

The cry of the Scrum Bolo Chihuahua.

And looming death has a way of focusing the mind.

So I thought back to something another camper had told me.

About the only possible way to escape the Scrum Bolo Chihuahua.

It was an option so repulsive, so distasteful, that he didn't even want to say it.

So he wrote it down.

YOU MUST KISS ANOTHER CAMPER ON THE LIPS!

And it is here that I must tell you that I was not the only person to wander into the woods that day.

There was one other.

CHAPTER
1
A Roomba with a View

Some detectives drive cars.

CARS

Others take cabs.

CABS

And some sit on their mother's Roomba.

Roomba

The Roomba is a robotic vacuum that roams across my mother's carpet in a pattern I have yet to discern.

As a result, I am frequently running into my polar bear.

And if you just said to yourself, *Wait, what polar bear? And by the way, who was the girl in that last chapter?* you must be one of the three or four people left in the world who did not read the prior volumes of my memoir.

So here, let me sum them up:

My name is Failure. Timmy Failure.

Me ← again

I am the founder, president, and CEO of the detective agency I have named for myself, Failure, Inc.

And I have solved most of the world's crimes.

I say "most" and not "all" only because the world is filled with seven billion people, and I cannot be everywhere at once.

Though I try.

Which can be hard on a Roomba that is ramming me into a chair.

Now the Roomba wouldn't be a problem if it had been programmed correctly. But that was the job of my business partner, Total.

My
← business
partner,
Total
(a.k.a. the
Polar
bear)

If you are ever tempted to hire a polar bear named Total, and you are ever tempted to make that polar bear a partner in your detective agency, and you are ever tempted to change the name of that agency from "Failure, Inc." to "Total Failure, Inc." in his honor, you should first know the following:

Polar bears sleep twenty hours a day.

And don't even think about complaining.

Because if you do, the bear will announce
it's time for hibernation and sleep for the next
three months.

I'd tell you more about the bear if I could.
But I can't.

Because my Roomba is headed out the front door.

CHAPTER 2

Going Old School

I live with my mother in the tallest apartment building in our city.

A building so massive that it has its own elevator.

So I ride on my Roomba out the front door of the apartment and head to the elevator, which is being held open by the building's doorman.

"Good morning, Timmy."

"Hello, Doorman Dave," I reply.

"Headed to school?" he asks.

"It's Saturday," I answer.

"Right," he answers. "Then you must be off to do your international spy work."

"I'm a detective, Doorman Dave. We solve crimes."

"I can't keep track of anything," he says.

The Roomba rotates and heads back toward the apartment door.

"I guess this is good-bye," I tell him.

"I thought you wanted to use the elevator," he says.

"Never question the Roomba," I answer.

I hear the elevator doors close behind me and see my mother standing in the apartment doorway.

"Good news," she says.

My idea of good news and my mother's idea of good news are never one and the same.

"Your old school is going to take you back," she says.

"That's terrible news," I answer.

She heads back inside the apartment and sits down at the dining-room table. I follow her on my Roomba.

"When did you hear all that?" I ask.

"I just got off the phone with Principal Scrimshaw," she says, glancing down at me. "And please get off my vacuum cleaner."

"What I want to know is how a school can kick out one of its students and then just suddenly decide to take him back," I say. "It shows no spine."

"Timmy, you have to go to school."

"Ordinary people have to go to school. I'm Timmy Failure."

Upon which the Roomba carries Timmy Failure under the dining-room table, where he runs into chairs.

"Timmy, get off that right now."

I get off the Roomba and crawl out from under the table.

"Timmy, we're lucky the school has agreed to do anything at all," she says, turning off the

Roomba and picking up a fallen chair. "You threw a tree stump through the principal's window."

"I fell," I answer.

"You still broke the window."

"Whose side are you on?" I ask.

"The side of keeping you in school. And it starts on Monday."

"Monday?" I answer. "That's not convenient."

"It's very convenient," she says. "Because it's the same day I start my job."

It's true. My mother has hit the big time.

KA-CHING

For she has got a job as a legal secretary.

Now I don't know what that is, but I know that the Defense Secretary is in charge of all our country's defense matters. So I assume my mother is in charge of all our country's legal matters.

And it's gone to her head.

"And I want to sign you up for a sport, Timmy. You could use some exercise. Move around a bit."

So I point to the Roomba.

"Doesn't count," she says.

CHAPTER
3

The Hitchhiker's Guide to the Grade School

My return to school was not filled with the marching bands and confetti I had hoped for.

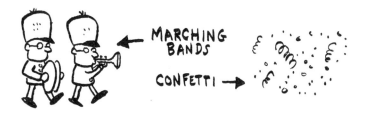

But rather, with the looming presence of Alexander Scrimshaw. Whose office was a dry and confetti-less place.

"Good morning, Timmy," says my principal.

"We meet again," I answer.

Scrimshaw presses his lips tightly together and straightens the piles of paper on his desk.

"Timmy, the school is happy to have you back. But as I explained to your mother, there are conditions."

"Of course," I answer.

My cooperation catches my foe off guard.

"Well, good," he says.

"And I have conditions as well," I say, pulling out a document prepared with diligence by my lawyer.

MY
← LAWYER

Scrimshaw rubs his eyes and folds his arms over his chest.

"Timmy, the school is placing you on academic and behavioral probation."

I do not know what that means, but I suspect it does not involve confetti.

"That means that you have to keep your grade point average above a C minus. And it means you have to behave. *Really* behave. Because if you don't . . ."

He sticks out his thumb and gestures toward the door.

"You'll hitchhike somewhere?" I ask.

SCRIMSHAW
HITCHHIKING

His eyes narrow to tiny, evil slits. "No, Timmy, you will."

He pauses as though listening for an ominous drumroll.

"You'll be permanently expelled."

I search for the humanity in those tiny, evil slits, but find none. Though as a hard-nosed detective, I expect none.

I look down at the sheet of ninety-five conditions I have asked my lawyer to prepare, intent on nailing it to Scrimshaw's door.

But I can't.

For it is filled with paw prints, pen marks, and grease stains.

I look back up at Scrimshaw.

"If you'll excuse me, I have a polar bear to fire."

CHAPTER 4

Blinded by the Light

It is a sunny day.

I am standing in a grass field.

And I am facing death.

It will come in the form of a hard little sphere.

And it will strike me in the head.

And I will die.

It is called Little League baseball. And it is what happens when your mother thinks you need an outdoor activity.

One filled with sunshine.

But sunshine is overrated.

For a detective works in the dark of night. Not the brutal light of day.

So I shield my eyes by pulling my cap entirely over my face.

And run around in circles.

"What are you doing?" yells Coach Drillashick from the dug-out.

"Moving target!" I yell. "Harder to hit!"

"Time out!" my coach yells.

Through the tiny holes in my cap, I see my coach walk out to right field, where I am still running in circles. He stands with hands on hips.

"Tim, stand still."

I stop running.

"How do you expect to catch the ball with your cap pulled over your eyes?" he asks.

"I don't. I see no need to jeopardize my future as a detective."

"Kid, it's just a ball."

"So is a cannonball."

"A baseball is not the same thing as a cannonball."

"Incorrect. They are each designed to cause harm."

"Can you two wrap it up out there?" shouts the umpire from behind home plate.

My coach looks toward the umpire, and back toward me.

"Okay, listen. If you see the big bad

cannonball coming your way, just hold up the big leather thing on your hand. It's a cannon-ball stopper."

I look at the leather thing on my hand and ponder how ineffective it would be against a cannonball.

The coach lumbers back to the bench. "Pray they don't hit it to the right," he says to one of the parents.

"Hmmph," says the parent.

And the game continues.

Or so I assume.

For the sun obliterates all.

And with nothing to see, I ponder life. And why it is my mother is trying to end mine.

And hear a loud CRACK.

For someone has struck the deadly sphere with a wooden stick.

Apparently on purpose.

And it is soaring my way.

At least according to my coach.

"You can get it, kid! You can get it! Charge in! Charge in!"

So I run as fast as I can toward home.

As in the one that has my bed.

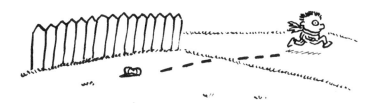

"Where are you GOING??" screams my coach.

But it is too late.

The detective has escaped.

CHAPTER 5

The Say Nay Kid

Bored by biology and beset by baseball, I spend my classroom time turning my classmates into baseball cards.

Feel free to copy these and store for handy reference.

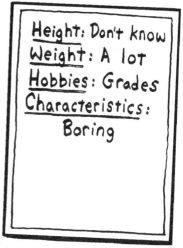

And here's one you probably won't want.

MOLLY
MOSKINS
(Annoying girl)

Occupation:
Criminal
Characteristics:
Mismatched
pupils
Smells like
tangerine
Pets: Female cat
named
Señor Burrito

And here's one you should probably crumple into a little ball and throw away.

CORRINA
CORRINA
(Thing from the
underworld)

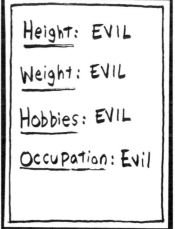

Height: EVIL

Weight: EVIL

Hobbies: EVIL

Occupation: Evil

"Oh, she's much cuter than that," says a voice from behind me.

It is my teacher, Mr. Jenkins. And he is hovering over my shoulder like a two-hundred-pound parrot.

"Corrina Corrina is the enemy of mankind," I explain. "And this portrait reflects the darkness of her soul."

"I see. So are you gonna do one of me?" he asks.

So I do.

"Timmy, I don't want to be too hard on you, because I know you're just rejoining us, but we have a nature project this semester that's half your overall grade. Did Mr. Scrimshaw discuss it with you?"

I do not know what he is talking about.

So I grab a piece of paper and quickly draft a nature project.

Jenkins smiles.

"I tell you what, Timmy. The bell's about to ring for the day, so I don't have time to explain it now. But I do have some paperwork about it that you can take home to your mom, and maybe the two of you can go through all the requirements together."

He hands me a thick folder filled with paper.

"After you read it through, let me know if you have any questions."

I flip through it. It is filled with five hundred thousand requirements and deadlines and deadlines and requirements.

So I make one more baseball card.

 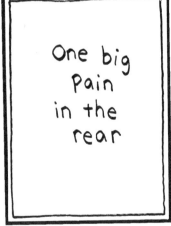

CHAPTER
6
Praying It Will End

"It's nice to finally have you back," says Rollo Tookus on our walk home from school. "It was strange having class without you."

"Charisma is a rare commodity," I answer from atop my polar bear (whom I have chosen to keep on the job, though on a probationary basis). "It's a wonder the school could function at all without me."

"You know, my grade point average actually went up while you were gone," he says. "A full tenth of a point. It's now 4.7. That's tied for the highest in the class with Corrina Corr—"

He catches himself.

"It's tied for the highest," he says.

"And poor Molly Moskins," he adds, changing the subject. "Here she waited all this time for you to return, and now *she's* leaving."

"Leaving? For where?"

"Peru. Her father got transferred for his work or something."

"Oh, please."

"Please what?"

"She wouldn't go to Peru because of her father."

"That's what she said."

"Bah! That little girl is probably smuggling stolen goods across the border as we speak. Shoes, spoons, the whole lot. I have half a mind to call border patrol on her now."

"Don't be silly, Timmy. She would never leave on her own. She'd miss her boyfriend too much."

"Boyfriend?" I answer, turning to face Rollo. "What boyfriend?"

"You didn't know?"

"Of course I didn't know. I have no interest in her personal life."

"Oh. Well, his name is Scutaro. Scutaro Holmes."

"Scutaro Holmes?" I respond, scratching the side of my head. "Why do I know that name?"

"He used to go to Reebler. Then he transferred to our school. He's the kid who won the detective contest."

"*I* won that contest!" I remind Rollo.

"Oh, right. Well, he's the kid who took home the prize money."

"*That* fraud?"

"What fraud?" asks a six-foot-tall praying mantis.

"Who are you?" I ask the oversize bug.

"Timmy," says a now-sheepish Rollo, "this is Scutaro Holmes. Scutaro is our official school mascot on game days."

"Mascot? Since when do we have a mascot?" I ask.

"Since I became class president and had the idea," interjects the praying mantis. "I wanted it to be a big scary bug. Everyone loves it!"

"It *is* pretty popular," says Rollo.

"Shut up, Rollo," I say, elbowing him in the ribs.

"And who are you?" asks Scutaro, reaching out and touching the top of my head with one of his bug legs. It is the kind of gesture that can trigger the predatory instinct of a polar bear.

If that polar bear had not just hidden behind a pole at the sight of a praying mantis.

I brush Scutaro's bug leg from atop my head.

"First, you know perfectly well who I am. And second, never touch a detective's head. We have reflexes we can't control."

Scutaro laughs. "Detective, huh? Right on. I had a lot of fun playing detective in that contest."

I feel my head about to explode.

"No one *plays* detective, Scutaro Holmes. It is a calling. A gift. A gift you don't have. Despite your last name. A name you sully, you ignoble charlatan."

"Whoa, whoa, whoa," he says, lifting four of his six bug legs in a conciliatory gesture. "Okay, first, you're *really* bringing down my school spirit. So 'boooo' to you for that. And second, I have no idea what you just said."

Before I can respond, Scutaro is surrounded by a cluster of cheering students, each of whom asks the pretend bug for a high five or fist bump. Scutaro pathetically obliges.

And then departs.

Idiots in tow.

"I leave this great institution for a short while," I say to Rollo, "and everything goes to pot."

Rollo says nothing.

I shake my head with contempt.

"Oh, how the mighty have fallen."

CHAPTER 7

War of the Mascots

"Timmy, you need to listen to this," says my mother, leafing through the paperwork that Jenkins gave me.

"I'm busy!" I yell from my room.

"This is important. *Come here.*"

I walk out of my room and stand in front of her.

"What are you doing?" she asks.

"I'm being Garbanzo Man."

"Who's Garbanzo Man?"

"My detective agency's mascot."

"And why are you doing that?"

"Because I want to wear it to school. The kids will love it."

"You are not wearing that to school."

"I will wear it, and I will wear it proudly."

"Timmy, we can discuss this later. Right now, we need to talk about the nature project. Did you look at what it requires?"

"Of course not. I haven't had time."

"Well, you better make time. You've got to visit parks, beaches, forests, everywhere. Then you have to collect all sorts of specimens—leaves, flowers, insects, rocks, feathers, fruits. And then you have to sketch each specimen and write about it in an extensive report. Timmy, this is a major time commitment."

I adjust my paper-bag mask.

"I'm thinking Garbanzo Man should have a sidekick," I say.

She yanks the bag off my head.

"Timmy. You. Are. On. Academic. Probation."

She punctuates each word with a poke to Garbanzo Man's newspaper-stuffed chest.

"Understand?"

"I understand. Scrimshaw has it in for me. His venal ways will get me yet."

"No, Timmy. This isn't about Scrimshaw. It's about you. And this project is half your grade. *Half*."

With no sense of timing, Garbanzo Man's sidekick, Rambling Rabbit, lumbers into the room.

My mom doesn't notice. I motion for him to go back out.

"And have you even thought about who your partner is going to be?" asks my mom.

"Partner?" I ask, still thinking of Rambling Rabbit.

" 'Each student will work with one other member of the class,' " reads my mom from the paperwork. " 'And the two students together will receive one grade.' "

I raise both my arms in triumph.

"Rollo Tookus!"

"Timmy," says my mom, shaking her head, "Rollo Tookus gets straight A's. *You* do not."

"So?"

"So this is one joint grade. Do you really think he wants to partner with you?"

"Rollo Tookus is my best friend. He'll do anything I say."

The doorbell rings.

"That must be him right now. Look at that. He's so smart he's telepathic."

So I answer the apartment door.
But it is not telepathic Rollo.

CHAPTER 8

Look What the Molly Dragged In

"Timmy!" chirps Molly Moskins. "Oh, I knew I'd get to see you before I leave! I knew it!"

"What are you doing here, Molly Moskins?"

"My cousins live in this same building! I visit all the time. And I noticed your last name on the tenant board in the lobby. Oh, it's you, Timmy Failure! It's you!"

She tries to hug me. I squirm free.

"Oh, and you've gotten so bigalicious!" she says, squeezing Garbanzo Man's bicep. "You must be lifting weights!"

"Stop touching me, Molly Moskins. And please leave. This is a private residence."

My mother mercifully interrupts.

"Hi, Molly. I'm Timmy's mother."

"Oh, hi, Ms. Failure. I think I met you once. I just wanted to say hi to Timmy before I leave."

"Well, that's nice of you. Where are you going?"

"My family's moving to Peru. But only for a few months. My dad has to work there."

"Oh, you must be so excited," says my mom.

"Oh, please," I mutter, imagining Molly smuggling shoes across the border.

"Oh, I am excited, Ms. Failure. But I'm sure gonna miss my cat."

"You can't take your cat?"

"No. The place we're going to doesn't allow cats. Poor Señor Burrito."

Señor Burrito... A cat as annoying as its owner

"Well, who's going to take care of him?" asks my mom.

Molly scans our apartment with her mismatched pupils.

I immediately see what is going on.

"Mother! Shut the door! Shut the door! She's casing the joint!"

"What?" asks my mother.

"Shut the door! Shut the door! She's scanning our room for valuables."

"Timmy, shush!" says my mother.

"It's okay, Ms. Failure. It's just a game Timmy and I play."

"A game?!" I shout, stunned at the felon's audacity.

My mother clamps her left hand over my mouth.

"Sorry," she says, turning to Molly. "So who's going to take care of him?"

"Well, Señor Burrito is a she, Ms. Failure. But we don't know who's gonna take care of her."

My mother places her other hand on her hip.

"You know, Molly," says my mother. "We don't have any animals. We could probably take care of her for a few months."

"Mother!" I yell, breaking free. "We have a fifteen-hundred-pound polar bear!"

1,500 LB. POLAR BEAR (currently dressed as rabbit)

"Shush!" she says again to me.

"Really, Ms. Failure? Would you really take care of her?"

"Sure," says my mother.

"Oh, thank you, Ms. Failure! Thank you! My mom can bring her by tonight!"

"Terrific," responds my mother. "And you have a great flight. And a great time in Peru. And take lots of pictures!"

My mother shuts the door. I reopen it.

"AND TAKE YOUR BOYFRIEND WITH YOU!"

CHAPTER 9

Miracle on 34th Street Playground

But Molly Moskins did not take her praying mantis boyfriend with her.

He stayed here.

And he is everywhere.

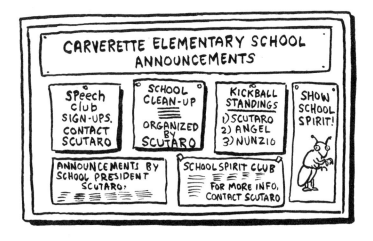

"Where does his need for attention end?"
I ask Rollo. "It's pathetic."

"Why are you dressed like that?" asks
Rollo.

"I'm Garbanzo Man. It's my agency's
mascot."

"Yeah, but why are you wearing it to
school?"

"To give the people what they want. If
the people want mascots, I'll give the people
mascots."

I hold up my hand to high-five a passing student. He declines.

"That's what you call respect," I say to Rollo. "Garbanzo Man's not just someone you high-five. He's too important for that."

I hold out my hand to fist-bump a female student. She screams.

"Look at that, Rollo. It's like I'm a rock star. Girls get so excited they can't control themselves."

Rollo stares at me in awe.

"I should probably start signing autographs," I muse. "Now, should I sign as Garbanzo Man or Timmy Failure?"

"You're Timmy Failure?" asks a deep voice from behind me.

"Why, yes, I—"

Before I can turn around, a young man has hoisted me over his shoulder.

"See what I mean, Rollo? The crowds love—"

"Shut up," says my fan.

He carries me to the tetherball courts on the far side of the playground and sets me down on the asphalt.

"Start playing tetherball," he says. "And act like you enjoy it."

"Tetherball? I can barely see out of—"

He hammers the ball with his fist. It soars far above my head and wraps itself around the pole.

"Well, that was useless," I say. "I can barely even—"

"What do you know about the Miracle report?" he interrupts, looking around to check for other students.

"The who?"

"Don't play dumb. You're supposed to be a detective."

I take the paper bag off my head. "I have no idea what you're talking about. But if this is official detective business, you'll need to know I don't work for free. First, I'll need—"

His eyes widen as he sees something over my shoulder. He slams the tetherball with his fist. It coils around the pole.

"I love it!" says the yard lady, Dondi Sweetwater, approaching us from the tennis courts. "Timmy Failure is playing sports! And here I thought you liked to spend lunchtime alone."

"He loves sports!" says my tetherball foe.

"I love sports," I echo him.

"Well, good," says Dondi. "Now go easy on him, Angel. You're bigger than he is."

And that's when I realize who this is.

Angel de Manzanas Naranjas. A legend in Carverette history. The only student ever asked to repeat a grade. *Twice.* Once because he ate the final exam. And once because he set fire to it.

He waits until Dondi is a safe distance away.

And whispers.

"The Miracle report is a nature report turned in a long time ago by some chick named Tracy Miracle. It got an A plus plus plus plus plus."

"Wow," I answer, stunned by the "plus plus plus plus plus."

"And it's filled with all types of stuff like rare birds and rare rocks and rare trees and rare sticks—"

"Rare sticks?" I ask.

 ← RARE STICKS?

"Shut up," says Angel. "It doesn't matter. The point is that whoever this weirdo Miracle was, she went out and did the best report, like, *ever*. And I got hold of it."

"How?"

"None of your business."

"And now you're going to copy it?"

"Not the whole thing, you idiot. That would be too obvious. Just parts. I figure that alone would be worth a B."

I hold my arms up like I'm still playing tetherball.

"So what do you need me for?" I ask.

"Because I lost it. And now I need to find it. *Fast*. Or else I'm gonna fail this grade again. And so are other people."

"Whoa, whoa, whoa," I say to Angel, dropping my arms to my side. "Other people? There are other people involved?"

"Keep your voice down," he growls. "All that stuff doesn't matter. And I don't need your stupid comments. I just need to know if you're gonna help me find it."

He leans his face menacingly into mine.

I keep my detective cool.

"Listen to me, Angel. That report is

contraband. Stolen goods. The kind of case that can get my detective license revoked faster than you can say 'Six times six is forty-eight.'"

6 × 6 = 48 (Basic Math)

I look around to make sure we're still alone.

"But I don't judge, Angel. Because I'm a detective. And I learned long ago that the moral failings of my fellow man are none of my concern."

Angel breathes into my face. It is the smell of dirty cash and cheap motels.

"No, Angel," I continue. "My concern is casework. And scoring the big one. That's detective talk for a case that can make or break an agency. And a case like this is that kind of case. The kind of case that comes along once in a generation. The kind of case that could catapult Total Failure, Inc. into the stratosphere of international detective work."

"Who cares about all that?" sneers Angel.

"I care," I answer. "Because I have drive. Guts. And the glint of greatness in my eyes. So I'll take your case, Angel de Manzanas Naranjas. But it's gonna cost you. Four times my normal rate. Sixteen bucks a day. Plus expenses. *Big* expenses. Like maybe a boat to Mexico. A *fast* boat. Because who knows how far the tentacles of this operation stretch."

"What are you, a nut?" says Angel. "I'm not paying you all that."

I lean one arm against the tetherball pole and smile.

"You don't have much of a choice, Angel."

Angel thinks.

"I could always just punch you in the face," he says.

I swallow hard.

"Okay," I answer. "But that wouldn't bring the Miracle report back."

Angel squeezes the tetherball with both hands, as though he's going to pop it.

"Fine," he says. "But I'm only agreeing to your stupid demands because I don't have a choice."

"But you *do* have a choice," says a female voice from behind me.

Startled, I wheel around.

"Because I'll take your case for free," she says.

CHAPTER 10

Wherein Garbanzo Man Taketh Over

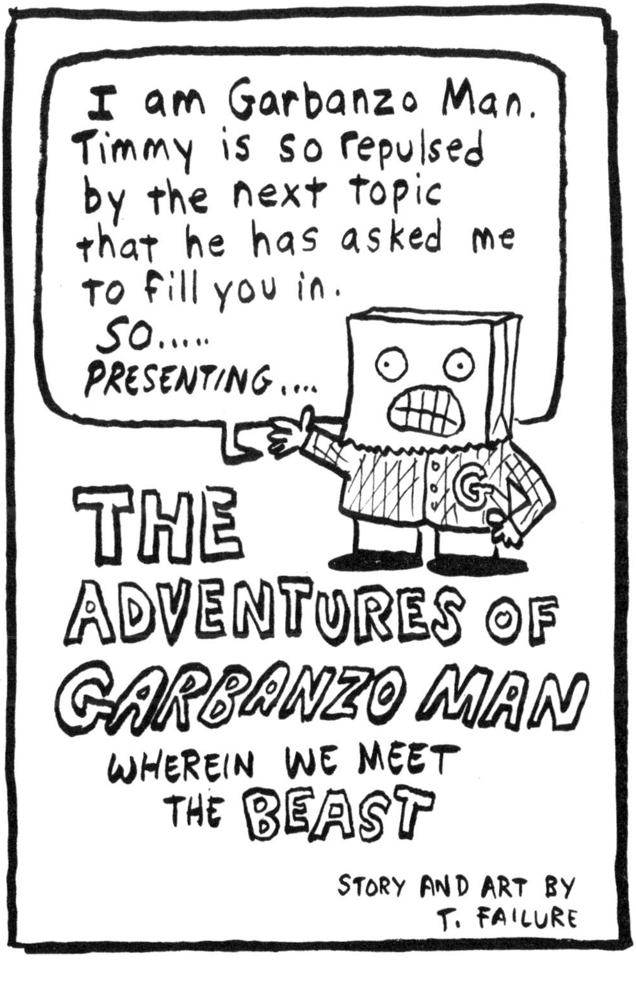

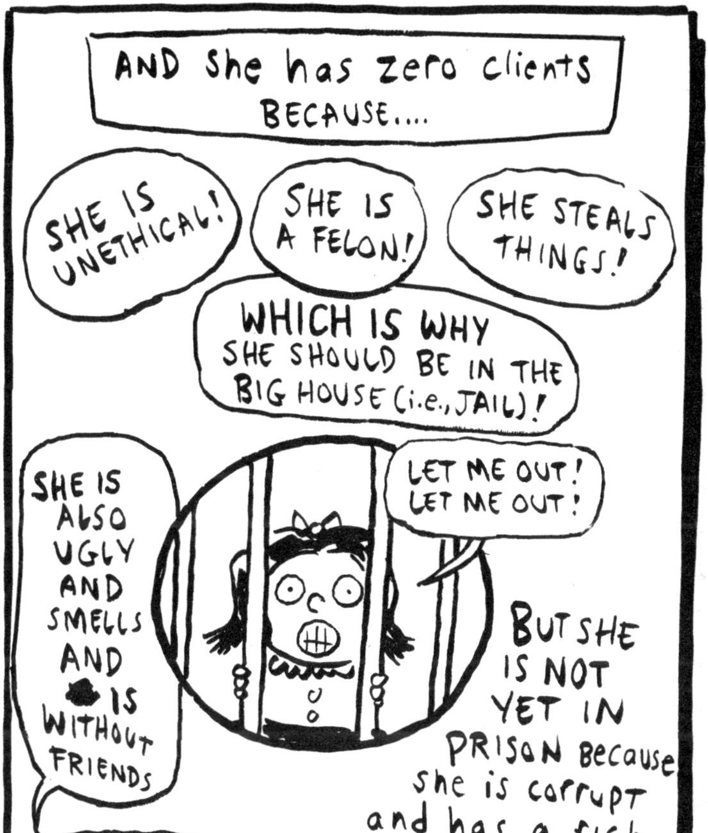

CHAPTER
II
Lo, the Knight Falls

So let us summarize.

My detective agency is on the verge of global domination.

Global riches.

Global fame.

And yet the gods are throwing me curveballs.

Curveballs in the form of nature reports.

Curveballs in the form of case-stealing detectives.

And curveballs in the form of curveballs.

"Now catch it," says Coach Drillashick. "Don't be afraid."

Yes, the same mother who thought it would be a great idea for me to be maimed in a baseball game now thinks it would be great for me to be maimed in extra practice sessions as well.

"Timmy, this is the only way you're going to get better!" shouts my mother from the safety of the bleachers. "And Coach Drillashick was nice enough to meet us here!"

"Here it comes," says Coach Drillashick, holding the baseball out in front of him.

"Now catch!" he says, tossing me the ball.

Which strikes me on the forehead.

"Oh, God," I scream. "I have brain damage."

I fall to the ground.

My mother walks over from the stands.

"Timmy, you're fine," she says, kneeling beside me.

"I've got brain damage. I can feel it. My superior brain is no more. Oh, God, the dream is over."

"Rela-a-a-a-ax," she says. "You're fine."

"Ohh, the humanity," I mutter.

"I barely threw it," offers Coach Drillashick, now kneeling over me as well.

"You fired it like a rocket!" I answer, my damaged brain temporarily reawakened. "Perhaps you should be renamed Coach Drill-A-Kid."

"Timmy, stop," says my mom.

"The dream is over," I mumble.

My mother looks at my coach. "I'm sorry, Rick. It's not your fault."

Rick? I say to myself. Since when does my sadistic coach have a first name? And since when does my mother use it?

"C'mon, Timmy," says my mother. "We'll

take you home. You've got homework you need to be doing anyway."

"Homework?" I answer. "Mother, please. The mind you knew as Timmy is no more."

She quickly discerns that I cannot move, and thus she lifts her fallen knight and carries his limp body from the battlefield.

"Proclaim that I served the queen well," I offer, my mind fading into hallucination.

She carries me across the field, her arms encircling my waist, my chin atop her shoulder. It is the first time I have been carried since I was a small child. And it is a delicate moment of beauty against an otherwise tragic backdrop.

"If this be the end," I whisper into her ear, "see to it that you carry on the Failure name."

"Hope to see you at the next game," interrupts Coach Drill-A-Kid, his glistening forearms folded boastfully over his hairy chest.

I lift my chin from my mother's shoulder and muster the strength for one last noble rejoinder.

"Ye shall be sued by nightfall."

CHAPTER 12

Matchmaker, Matchmaker, Make Me a Wretch

Despite my life-threatening condition, my mother makes me go to school.

Early.

"Because," she says, "you need to make sure you have a partner for that nature project."

So I stumble to school, my consciousness fading.

I find Rollo Tookus sitting on the ground outside the locked classroom door.

"Hey, Timmy," he says, looking up from his math book. "What are you doing here? You never come early. And what happened to your head?"

"You need to be my partner," I tell him.

"Your partner on what?" he asks.

"Please, Rollo. No dumb questions. I've suffered a grievous injury to my bean."

"But I don't know what you're talking about."

"What do you *think* I'm talking about, Rollo? The nature project."

"Oh, that."

"Yes, that. And I'll need you to do most of the work."

"Why?"

"Because I'm battling the Beast."

THE BEAST

"I have no idea what that means," says Rollo.

So I pull out her baseball card.

CORRINA
CORRINA
(Thing from the
underworld)

"Her," I say, pointing.

"Oh," he answers. "That doesn't really look like her."

"Who cares, Rollo? *Focus.*"

"Focus on what?"

"The nature project. Now if you need help on it, you can contact me. But I'd prefer that you didn't. I'm at a pivotal moment in my professional career."

"Timmy, I think you better talk to Mr. Jenkins."

"Jenkins? Why?"

"Because I already have a partner."

"Who?"

"Nunzio Benedici."

"The kid who shoves eraser tips up his nose?"

NUNZIO
BENEDICI
(SHOVER OF ERASER
TIPS UP HIS NOSE)

"Yes," says Rollo. "He's my partner."

"Well, just tell him he's no longer your partner. Adios. Vamoose."

"I would," says Rollo. "But I didn't pick him."

"Who did?"

"Mr. Jenkins."

"Since when does our teacher pick the partners?"

"Since always. That's the way it works, Timmy. If you don't like it, you better talk to him."

So I pound on the locked classroom door.

"He's not in there," says Rollo, staring again at his math book.

"Where is he?"

"Staffroom. He likes to drink coffee in there before class. Decaf. Cream. No sugar."

"You know way too much about the sub-culture of this institution," I say to Rollo. "Find some hobbies."

So I march down the hall toward the door marked STAFF ONLY and bang on it with my fist.

But Jenkins doesn't answer. My unprincipled principal does.

"What do you think you're doing?" says Alexander Scrimshaw. "And what in heaven's name happened to your head?"

"I'm looking for Jenkins."

"*Mr.* Jenkins," he corrects me. "And this is the staffroom. Can you read?"

He points to the STAFF ONLY stenciled on the door.

"But I have to talk to him."

"Then you'll wait until he gets to class. Now, leave. You're on thin ice, Failure."

But as he says it, the door opens wider and Mr. Jenkins steps out.

"Well, hello, Timmy," he says.

He turns to Scrimshaw.

"It's okay, Alex. I'm on my way to class anyway. I can talk to him."

He turns back to me.

"What is it, Timmy? And what happened to your head? Are you okay?"

"Rollo says he can't be my partner on the nature project. He says you pick them."

"Ah, yes," says Mr. Jenkins. "I was going to talk to you about that this morning, in fact. There was a bit of a problem."

"There's a big problem," I answer. "Rollo's not my partner."

Scrimshaw glares at me with his small, soulless eyes.

"Well, yes," says Mr. Jenkins. "But there's nothing I can do about that. I picked those partners long ago, and both of them are well into the work."

"So what am I supposed to do?" I plead. "Work alone? This is *half* my grade!"

"No, no, Timmy. You have to have a partner. And that was the problem. You see, originally, there was an even number of students in the class and so everyone had a partner. But now, with Molly Moskins leaving for Peru, she's left her partner—well, partnerless."

"So Molly's partner is now my partner?"

"Yes. That's how it has to work."

"So who's my partner?" I ask.

The school bell rings. Students begin rushing to class.

"Well . . ." He hesitates, looking over his shoulder toward Scrimshaw.

"Who is it?" I ask.

"Tell him," says Scrimshaw.

"Well, Timmy, I know you don't . . . I mean, I tried to—"

"Let me," says Scrimshaw.

Scrimshaw steps forward, resting one hand on Mr. Jenkins's shoulder. And smiles.

"Your partner is Corrina Corrina."

CHAPTER 13

Beauty (of a Plan) and the Beast

"Scrimshaw thinks he's got me. But he doesn't got me," I say, unconcerned with good grammar and aware that my polar bear won't correct me.

"Are you listening to me?" I ask.

Total grunts.

"At least you make a nice pillow," I say.

It is our first official Total Failure, Inc. meeting in our new office—the balcony of our apartment. And it is a fittingly high altitude for the ascending fortunes of the company.

HUGE BUILDING

US

RANDOM BIRDS

"So Scrimshaw thinks I'll do something stupid if I'm paired with the Beast. Throw a fit. Toss a tree stump. Something that will get me kicked out of school. But I won't. My detective brain is too savvy for that."

Total yawns. His expanding lungs lift me like a rolling wave.

"So then he thinks I'll do something bad academically. Something that Corrina Corrina will be witness to because now we're partners. So she'll be like his little spy. Then she'll run and spill the beans on my poor contribution to the partnership. And *KABOOM*, he'll cut Corrina Corrina loose from me, give her an A, give me an F, and kick me out of school. You see how that works?"

Total is asleep. I continue talking.

"But you know what, Total? None of that is going to happen. Because that's where the Miracle case comes in."

The intercom in the apartment beeps, followed by the muffled voice of Doorman Dave.

"There's a Rollo Tookus in the lobby here to see you."

I get off Total's stomach and press the TALK button. "Tell him to hang on a minute, Doorman Dave. I'm in a meeting."

I return to the balcony and pace.

"You see, Total, the Miracle case is the key to everything. Because if I find that report before Corrina Corrina does, I won't have to do a bit of work. I'll just copy from it like Angel and everyone else. And what will Corrina Corrina be able to do about it? She won't know I have it. All she'll see is me contributing solid work. Nothing she can complain to Scrimshaw about because—"

The intercom beeps again.

"Mr. Tookus says he's tired of waiting in the lobby."

"Oh, good gosh," I say to Total. "Is there no respite from that round interloper?" I press the TALK button again. "Fine, Doorman Dave. Send him up. But tell him he's disturbing a Fortune 500 meeting."

I turn back to Total.

"By the way, I haven't even mentioned the fact that finding the Miracle report would put Total Failure, Inc. on the front page of every newspaper in the country. And that could mean a bonus for you. Maybe even an increase in your chicken nugget ration."

Total's right eye opens at the mention of food. Seeing none, it closes.

"Now the only possible complication is if Corrina Corrina gets that Miracle report first. Because who knows what that charlatan would do with it. Copy from it herself? Hide it from me? Who can say? So we can't let that happen."

"Can't let what happen?" asks a voice from the apartment.

I turn and see Rollo in my living room.

"Don't you ever knock?" I ask.

"Door was open," he says. "Hey, nice apartment."

"The door was open?" I shout. "The cat will get out!"

"What cat?" asks Rollo.

The intercom beeps again.

"Timmy, I've got a cat down here," announces Doorman Dave. "Know anything about it?"

"Way to go," I say to Rollo.

"I didn't do anything," he responds.

I turn back to the intercom.

"I'll come down and pick her up, Doorman Dave."

"It may not be quite that easy," answers the doorman.

"What do you mean?"

Doorman Dave clears his throat.

"She's stuck in the vending machine."

CHAPTER 14

Not F.I.T. for Duty

"It figures that the cat of a felon like Molly Moskins would be a felon herself," I say to Rollo as I return with the cat. "She was going to rob that vending machine blind."

"How'd you get her out?"

"I had to put in coins and order her like a bag of Fritos. You owe me a dollar twenty-five."

"It wasn't my fault she escaped," objects Rollo. "And why do you have Molly's cat, anyway?"

"Because she couldn't take it with her to Peru. I guess they're anti-cat."

"Gato," says Rollo.

"What's that?"

"That's how you say 'cat' in Spanish," he says.

"Good for you, Rollo," I answer. "Now if you're done, I'm in the midst of a big TFI case."

" 'TFI'?"

"Total Failure, Inc. It's how we're branding ourselves now. Like how Kentucky Fried Chicken became KFC."

"Impressive," says Rollo.

"I know," I answer. "We even had a logo designed."

I point to the sign on the wall.

"That says 'FIT,' not 'TFI,' " says Rollo.

"Yes, I know, Rollo. There was a typo."

"Kinda makes you look like you're a fitness center or something," he adds.

"Drop it, Rollo. The signage was the responsibility of my business partner. And it's a very sore subject."

I glance over at my business partner. He is suitably ashamed.

"So what's the big TFI case?" he asks.

"I can't tell you."

"You always tell me about your cases."

"Not this one, Rollo. It's dirty business."

"Sounds serious."

"It is serious. And it's best you know nothing."

"Fine," he says. "I gotta go home anyway. I just wanted to see your new place and ask if you're still gonna spend the night at my house next week."

"Can't," I answer. "My mother won't let me."

"You asked her already?"

"No need. She wants me to focus on school. If you recall, a certain somebody refused to be my nature project partner."

"That wasn't my fault," objects Rollo.

"Regardless, I will now have to work ten times harder than I would have had to otherwise. Surely, you can see the unfairness in that."

"Fine. But it's not my fault," says Rollo.

"Fine. It's not your fault," I answer as the Roomba enters the room.

"What's that?" asks Rollo.

"It's a vacuum cleaner. And it's how I get around."

"Ooh, I want to try!" he says.

Rollo sits on the Roomba.

There is a loud *crack* as a chunk breaks off and the Roomba stops moving.

Rollo has killed the Roomba.

"Okay, *that's* my fault," he mutters.

CHAPTER 15

Look Backward, Angel

My personal and professional life on the line, I submit a detailed questionnaire to Angel de Manzanas Naranjas to try to elicit the details of what exactly happened to the Miracle report.

Where is the last place you saw the Miracle report? (Please provide precise location. If within a building, please provide city, street address, and postcode.)

_____
_____
_____
_____

When did you last have the Miracle report in your possession? (Please provide date/time. Time should be to nearest minute.)

_____
_____
_____
_____

Who is the last person other than you to see the Miracle report? (Please provide name, height, weight, eye color, hair color, and date of birth.)

_____
_____
_____
_____

Angel's answers are less than informative.

Where is the last place you saw the Miracle report? (Please provide precise location. If within a building, please provide city, street address, and postcode.)

DON'T KNOW.

When did you last have the Miracle report in your possession? (Please provide date/time. Time should be to nearest minute.)

DON'T KNOW.

Who is the last person other than you to see the Miracle report? (Please provide name, height, weight, eye color, hair color, and date of birth.)

You're weird.

So I try to simplify the questions.

Where is the last place the Miracle report was seen?

☐ On Earth.
☐ Somewhere else.
☐ None of the above.

When did you last have the Miracle report in your possession?

☐ This century.
☐ Not this century.
☐ I can't tell time.

Please describe the last person or persons to see the Miracle report.

☐ They had a head.
☐ They were headless.
☐ You've confused me.

But Angel doesn't answer.

Because he doesn't have to.

Because instead of hiring the brilliant Timmy Failure to be his detective, he has hired this person:

And while she is not yet in prison, the Beast was desperate and unethical enough to work for free.

And so now she has a client.

But that is of little consequence.

For I am going to solve the Miracle case whether or not I am the detective of record.

For solving it means doing well on my half of the nature report. And establishing TFI as the preeminent detective agency in the world.

Though that will be harder without the cooperation of Angel de Manzanas Naranjas.

Who, when asked in my questionnaire to provide any additional information he could in the extra blank lines on the back, filled it in as follows:

CHAPTER
16

I Ain't Gonna Work for Timmy's Ma No More

I am sitting in the conference room of my mother's law firm. And I feel the power coursing through my veins.

"Get your feet off that table right now," my mother barks.

"What's the big deal?" I ask. "You're the boss."

"I'm a legal secretary, Timmy. And I just started working here."

I see a white-haired man in khaki trousers walk past the glass wall of the conference room.

"Tell the little man to bring us coffee," I suggest to my mother.

My mom claps her hand over my mouth.

"Good morning, Mr. Melvin," she says to the passing man.

"Good morning, Ms. Failure," he answers.

She waits until the man passes and then releases her hand.

"Well, that was unprofessional," I say. "Covering my mouth like I'm a child. You've been doing that a lot lately."

"That was the senior partner in the law firm," my mother whispers from behind gritted teeth.

"So does he not know how to make coffee?" I ask.

She covers my mouth again.

"Timmy, I just brought you in here on a

Saturday because I needed to get some work done. Now if you're bored, why don't you get something to eat from the break room? I think there's a leftover donut in there."

I stand up and stare out the glass wall that separates the conference room from the office lobby.

"Maybe we should fire some people," I say.

She grabs me by the back of the shirt and pulls me back into the seat.

"Better yet, you stay here," she orders. "And *I'll* get the donut."

My mother exits. And while she is gone, I stare out the large conference room window that overlooks the city.

And I raise my arms in triumph.

"Though I look down at you from the international headquarters of Total Failure, Inc.," I
proclaim, "I give you my word that I, Timmy
Failure, shall always strive to be kind to the
little people."

The conference room door swings open.

"Can I help you?" asks a bald man.

As he says it, my mother walks up to the
conference room with a napkin and donut.

"I'm so sorry," says my mother. "He's my
son. I just needed to do some work and—"

The bald man cuts her off.

"A law office is not a day-care center," he says.

"Of course," she says. "I'm very sorry."

The man smiles with pursed lips and walks off.

My mother looks at me. She is not mad. She is worried.

"We'll fire him first," I say.

CHAPTER 17

I'm Your Number One Fan

I have found the world's largest bug. And I want to trap him in a jar.

"I have sixty-five different leaves collected for the nature report," says Scutaro. "How about you, Timmy?"

"Ask Rollo. I don't talk to people in costumes."

"I have forty-one," says Rollo. "And twenty-three different rocks."

"I have twenty-six rocks," says Scutaro.

"How many rocks and leaves do you have, Timmy?" asks Rollo.

"A lot," I reply.

"I heard you had none," says Scutaro.

"I don't talk to bugs," I answer.

"I heard it from Corrina Corrina," says Scutaro. "She's afraid you're gonna ruin her grade."

I turn and face the bug.

"Don't you have a useless school club you can form?" I ask Scutaro.

Scutaro laughs.

"Maybe *you* could form a school club," says Scutaro. "The disturbing mascot club. I heard you were walking around as some guy called Garbage Man. That's really funny. Though odd."

GARBAGE MAN?

"It's *Garbanzo* Man," I tell Scutaro. "And it was a lot more popular than the sad costume *you're* wearing."

"Praying Mantis rocks!" yells a passing student.

Scutaro holds out four of his bug legs for a high five. The student high-fives all four of them in quick succession.

"I love it when they do that," says Scutaro.

"Pathetic," I mutter.

Scutaro turns back toward me. "Well, I'm sure Garbage Man has his fans, too."

I don't answer.

"Like the one behind you," says Scutaro.

I turn to look, wary of a possible trick.

And see a person.

But it is not a fan.

CHAPTER 18

It's the Beastie Girl

I was not there when Esmeralda first met the Hunchback of Notre Dame.

Or when Dorothy confronted the Wicked Witch of the West.

But I was there when I, Timmy the Great, came face-to-face with the Beast.

And it was awkward.

"I don't think we've ever really talked," she says. "But we probably have a lot in common. You have a detective agency, right?"

"HA!" I shout, turning my back on the Bad-Eyed Lady of the Lowlands.

"Tell her we can skip the pleasantries," I say to Rollo.

"You tell her," says Rollo. "She's right next to you."

"Rollo, she's just delivered an opening salvo directed at me, my global reputation, and my agency. Tell her I will talk through you."

"I didn't mean anything by that," says the Damsel of Darkness.

"She is well aware of my agency," I say to Rollo.

Rollo looks at the Beast. "He thinks you are well aware of—"

The Beast cuts him off. "I can hear him, Rollo."

"Awww, the two professional detectives are fighting," says Scutaro the Praying Mantis.

"Timmy, I just want to see when you can meet. I think we're a little behind on the nature project. Molly and I have done a fair amount, but I should probably catch you up so that—"

"Tell her that these are dark days," I say to Rollo. "Days of famine and pestilence. But that I, Timmy the Great, shall persevere."

Rollo shrugs. "Timmy, she's just trying to—"

"Tell her," I urge Rollo.

"Uh, these are dark days, Corrina Corrina. Days of—"

"I got it, Rollo," says the Mistress of Malevolence. "Listen, I'm sorry if I offended you, Timmy. I didn't mean to. But we need to work together. So if you'd like to meet, I have sort of my own office. Well, it's not really an office. It's just really a place my dad owns downtown."

The bank, I think.

The heart of darkness.

The Death Star.

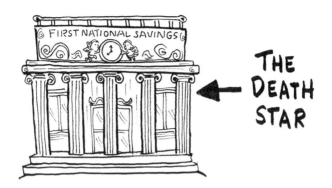

THE
DEATH
STAR

But I remain silent, my back turned.

"Aw, kiss and make up, you two," says Scutaro the Bug.

"So if you'd like to meet," she repeats, then stops and turns to Rollo.

"Rollo, if Timmy's not going to talk to me, will you please tell him that I can meet him tomorrow and that the bank is located at 505 San—"

I whip around.

"I shall be there at high noon," I say.

She stares back at me in awe. Her dark eyes like black holes from which no light can escape.

"Yaaaaay!" cheers Scutaro the Praying Mantis. "Now kiss her on the lips."

So I pull off his right antenna.

"That shows very poor school spirit," he says.

CHAPTER 19

Let's Spend the Night at Rollo's

"Rollo Tookus's mother just called," says my mom. "Why did you tell him that I wouldn't let you spend the night at his house?"

"Because it's true."

"I never said you couldn't spend the night."

"Well, you should. It's a bad idea."

"Why is it a bad idea?"

"Because he's irresponsible and unpredictable."

My mother laughs. "Rollo?" she says. "He's the sweetest kid I know."

"Oh, really?" I answer. "Well, maybe you didn't know that he broke your vacuum cleaner."

"Rollo broke the Roomba?"

"Yes."

"Well, I'm sure it was an accident."

"No," I answer. "It was no accident. I saw him whack it with a mallet. I told him to stop, but he was quite frenzied."

ROLLO'S FRENZIED ATTACK

"Somehow I doubt that," says my mother. "I think the bigger issue is why you don't want to spend the night there."

"There is no bigger issue, Mother. It's unwise. Please be a responsible parent and decline the invitation."

My mother kneels beside me and puts both her arms around my waist.

"Timmy," she whispers into my ear. "It's okay. It's okay to get homesick."

"Absurd!" I shout, breaking free from her arms. "Detectives do not get homesick! What do you think I am—*a little kid*?"

"Well, there was that time you stayed at your grandmother's and you got really sad and you called and said—"

"I was not homesick! I told you—the pillows were too hard! I do not like hard pillows!"

"All right, all right," she says. "Calm down."

"Not liking hard pillows is *hardly* the same as being homesick," I add.

"Fine, Timmy. I'll drop it. I just thought that since I have a date this weekend, it might be easier if you went to Rollo's and I didn't have to get you a babysitter."

"A *date*?" I reply. "You have a *date*?"

"Yes."

"I don't remember giving this my blessing," I reply.

"I didn't know I needed your approval."

"Well, shouldn't I at least meet him first?"

"You have," she says.

"I haven't met anyone," I answer.

"It's Rick," she says. "Your baseball coach. He's coming over on Saturday."

← WHAT THIS DEBACLE COULD LOOK LIKE

I stare dumbfounded at my mother.

"I shall spend the night at Rollo's," I say.

And pause.

"And he better not have hard pillows."

CHAPTER 20

Just Click Your Paws Together Three Times

My mother's betrayal of me is so profound that I cannot sleep.

"You are dating the man who tried to maim me," I told her just before bed. "Think of the message that sends. He'll think it's a *reward*."

But she would not listen to reason.

So I wander out into the cool night air of the balcony, where I find my business partner on his hind legs, staring out over the railing.

It is something he does more and more ever since he discovered the ice rink.

The rink is only a few blocks away. And it is old and run-down.

But the side of the building that faces our high-rise contains a hand-painted mural. A mural of a snow-covered village that can clearly be seen from our apartment.

And it reminds Total of home.

"It's okay," I say, putting my arm around his large waist. "One day we'll make so much money that I'll build you your *own* ice rink."

I point to the ice rink.

"And it will be *way* better than that old one."

Total's nose twitches. It is something he does when he's hungry.

And when he's sad.

So I climb up his long neck and sit atop his head.

And we stare at the ice rink together.

CHAPTER
21
High Noon

I arrive at the Beast's office as a man at the peak of his professional power.

And that means looking professional.

So I wear a suit.

But it is owned by Rollo's father.

I try wearing a tie as well, but I do not know how to tie one. So I add a bit of flair by simply wrapping it around my waist.

And when I finally see the Beast, I can tell she is impressed.

"Good afternoon," I say.

"Hello, Timmy," she answers.

I smile and point to my apparel. "The suit makes the man."

"I see," she responds. "Do you always dress like that to study?"

"Interesting place," I answer, coolly ignoring the query. "May I have a look around?"

"All right," she says, "but there's not much to see. May I take your, uh, coat?"

I hand her my coat and tie and stroll through the room. It is a large, cavernous expanse of marble, divided in two by an ornate wooden wall that once separated the bank tellers from the customers.

"Decent amount of space," I say.

"It's big," she answers.

"But empty," I note.

"I guess," she says.

So I take a chance.

"And where is your . . . equipment?" I ask.

"Equipment?" she replies.

"Detective equipment," I answer. "I'm just curious."

"I don't really have any," she says, "other than a pair of binoculars my dad bought me."

Of course.

She is onto me.

She knows that I am only here to do surveillance.

So she has hidden everything from view.

And she abruptly changes the subject.

"Should we start working?" she asks, pointing to numerous sheets of paper that have been spread out on the marble floor. There are drawings of leaves and trees and birds.

The boring stuff

"Of course," I answer. "It is why I am here. You will have my full cooperation."

I look around, determined to see where she has hidden her equipment, her files, her evidence room. But I see nothing.

"We really have a lot to do," she says. "And I can only use this place until my dad gets back in a couple of hours."

I try to continue the conversation, if only to stall for time.

"Ah, yes. Your father," I say. "And where is the gentleman?"

"The gentleman? Why are you talking so funny, Timmy? Well, the gentleman—my dad—is somewhere downtown. He drops me off here when he has business in the area. He owns a lot of buildings that he has to sort of manage, I guess. Like this one. I just mostly use it to play with friends."

HA, I think. Play.

I stand in the center of the most nefarious operation in the detective world, and she wants me to believe it's for play.

ILLUSTRATION OF HER FAR-FETCHED ACCOUNT

YAY!

It is thus clear that she will reveal nothing.

So I raise the stakes.

"May I use the gentlemen's room?" I ask.

"Sure," she says. "It's in the back. Want me to show you where?"

"No," I quickly answer.

Perhaps too quickly.

So I take a breath.

"I can find it myself," I say.

I saunter calmly down a long marble hall, a tight-lipped smile pasted to my face. And there, I see two toilet doors. And just beyond them, a set of double doors.

I look behind me to make sure I am not being followed and dart past the toilets to the double doors.

Where I hesitate momentarily. And then push them open.

And find a long, wooden corridor.

That ends in a large walk-in safe.

Which is open.

Bingo.

The center of the Death Star.

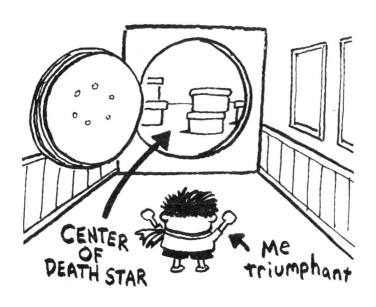

CENTER OF DEATH STAR

Me triumphant

The safe is filled with dozens of cardboard boxes.

Aha! I think. Her case files. Her evidence. *Perhaps even the Miracle report itself.*

I greedily tear the lid off the first box. It is filled with documents. First National this. First National that. Of course. It's not going to be that easy. She's buried her detective agency records deep within the bank records. I begin tossing the paper wildly out of the boxes.

Until I hit a file marked CONFIDENTIAL.

It is too thick to take with me. But it is a contingency I have planned for.

So I reach for the disposable camera I borrowed from my mother.

And realize it is in my jacket pocket. *The jacket I have given to the Beast.*

I begin shoving the documents frantically back in the box and sprint back down the maze of halls.

"Excuse me, Corrina Corrina," I say, breathing heavily. "But may I please have my jacket?"

"Are you okay?"

"Yes. Of course."

"Are you leaving?" she asks.

"Don't be silly. I'm just using the facilities."

She pauses.

"And you need your jacket for that?"

"Yes," I answer, almost out of breath, "I do."

She stares blankly at me.

So I think fast.

"If you must know, the toilet seat is rather chilly."

BRRRRRRR

She wrinkles up her nose like she has smelled something unpleasant. When she hands me back my jacket, she holds it as far out from her body as she can.

"Thank you," I politely say.

I zigzag back through the network of corridors until I get to the safe. Once there, I look back to make sure the Beast did not follow, and I reach for the camera in my jacket pocket.

And it moves.

And meows.

"Señor Burrito!" I snarl.

I should have known better than to leave the suit jacket lying unguarded on my bed at home. That felonious cat probably saw an opportunity to steal a wallet.

The cat meows repeatedly.

"Shhhhh," I say, "shhhhhh," as I push her head gently back into my pocket.

And hear a voice from back in the large room.

"You okay in there, Timmy?"

I want to answer. But I can't. Because if I do, she'll be able to tell that I'm nowhere near the bathroom.

So I remain quiet. Too quiet.

"Oh, gosh," I hear her say. "Did you get locked in the bathroom? Those doors really stick. If you can hear me, Timmy, hang on. I'm coming."

Oh, God, I think. She can't find me in the safe.

She cannot find me in the safe.

So I leap up.

But as I leap up, Señor Burrito leaps out.

Out of my pocket and up the wall of safety deposit boxes that line the safe.

"No, you criminal feline, this is no time to steal!" I shout, reaching for the cat.

"Wrowr!" she cries as I try to grab her, scratching my wrist with her claw.

"OW!" I yell.

"Timmy, are you okay? Are you okay?" The footsteps approaching me quicken.

I have no time. I grab the file marked CONFIDENTIAL and run down the hallway. But the hall is strewn with documents I have hurled from the boxes. So I reach down and grab as many as I can and shove them into my suit pocket.

And as I do, I hear the footsteps coming closer.

So I leave the rest of the documents and race to the end of the hall and turn sharply toward the bathrooms.

I've done it! I will beat her to the bathrooms!

And as I make the turn, my foot gets caught on the bottom of my oversize suit jacket.

And I trip.

And fall face-first.

And a file marked CONFIDENTIAL flies out of my hand and slides down the slick marble hall.

Coming to rest at two feet.

The feet of Corrina Corrina.

I look up at the men's room door.

"So *this* is where the bathroom is."

CHAPTER 22

Pillow Talk

"So what did you do next?" asks Rollo.

"I did what any smart detective would do. I grabbed the cat and fled."

"So you didn't end up working on the project at all?"

"No."

"Oh, she's gonna be so mad. She's gonna tell Scrimshaw."

"Of course she's gonna tell Scrimshaw. But who cares?"

"Scrimshaw's gonna care."

"Rollo, I didn't agree to spend the night at your house so we can talk about *school*. Please. You'll bore me right to sleep."

Rollo rolls over in his sleeping bag.

"Okay," he says. "Let's talk about something else. Do you like ghost stories?"

"Ghost stories? No."

"But they're fun."

"For little kids, maybe. I'm beyond that."

"Well, have you ever heard the story of the Scrum Bolo Chihuahua?"

"Is it a ghost story?"

"No. It's a giant Chihuahua story."

"Sounds ridiculous."

"It's not ridiculous. It's *scary*. He eats kids."

"Fine," I answer. "But let me plug this in first."

I reach into my overnight bag and pull out a Mr. Froggie night-light, which I plug into the wall.

"What do you need that for?" he asks.

"It's called a night-light, Rollo. My mother bought it. Do you think *I* would buy a Mr. Froggie night-light?"

"Yeah, but why do you need it? Do you not like the dark?"

"Oh, good gosh, Rollo. Do you seriously think Timmy Failure gets s*cared*? Have you forgotten who you're talking to? I've faced death without flinching."

"Then why do you need it?"

"*Because*, Rollo, detectives like me have large brains that never stop. Not even in the middle of the night. And when my large brain generates a brilliant idea, I need a light so I can write it down."

"Oh."

"So tell your silly dog story. And it better be brief. You're starting to bore me already."

"Oh, it's not boring," says Rollo. "It's terrifying."

"So tell it, already," I say.

"Okay, so I don't know if this really happened or not, but my brother's friend's cousin apparently knows one of the people involved, and he swears it really—"

"TELL THE DUMB STORY ALREADY!"

"Okay, okay, okay . . . So there's this camp, right? Camp Monkeychuck. It's about forty-five miles from here. It's real. Do you know it?"

"I don't know if I know it. Just go on."

"Well, like twenty years ago or so, there were these two campers from the camp. Little kids. Like our age. And they got lost in the woods next to the camp."

"This sounds totally fake, Rollo."

"Listen, listen. So they're missing, right? They don't show up for meals. They don't show up for activities. So the camp sends out this search party to find them. And they search for, like, a week. Or it might have been ten days. And they find absolutely nothing. No crumbs. No flashlights. No sleeping bags—"

"Speaking of which," I interrupt. "I cannot sleep on this pillow. It's way, way too hard."

"Take mine," says Rollo, handing me his pillow. "I don't even need a pillow. I can sleep on anything."

"Gross," I say. "It smells like you."

"Sorry," he says. "It's all I have. Now, where was I? Oh, right, they're searching for the missing campers. Okay, so they're searching. Like really hard. Under rocks. In rivers. Everywhere. And they never find them—"

"This pillow's just as hard, Rollo," I interrupt, hitting it with my fist.

"I told you—it's all I have, Timmy. But listen to the story. It gets good."

Rollo's voice descends to a throaty whisper. The Mr. Froggie night-light projects his large shadow on the opposite wall.

"So the next year, the camp is filled with all new campers, right? I guess the camp hushed up what happened to the prior campers, so nobody knew. And these new kids go into the woods for a campfire or something. Maybe not a campfire. But it was for something."

"Does it matter, Rollo?" I ask. "This is getting really, really boring."

"Right. I guess it doesn't. But so the kids are all sitting there in the woods, right? And all of a sudden, they hear this crazy deep *BARK*! Like from a dog! And they look up. And they see a GIANT FLYING DOG! *THE SCRUM BOLO CHIHUAHUA!* And it swoops down right over their heads! And it opens its jaws really wide. But get this—it doesn't eat them! It just drops something right in the middle of them. *PLOP!* And the kids are thinking, well, maybe it's a doggie treat or something that the giant dog wants to share with them."

"THIS IS VERY, VERY STUPID, ROLLO. YOU SHOULD PROBABLY STOP RIGHT NOW."

"But it's no treat," Rollo says, his eyes wide, his shadow enormous.

"It's the bones of the two missing—"

But I don't hear the rest of it. Because my pillow becomes unbearable.

So I bolt out the front door with my sleeping bag in tow and disappear into the cool dark night.

And as I run, tears streaming down my cheeks from the sting of the bitter wind, I am certain of only one thing—that I will never hear of anything more ridiculous, anything more revolting, anything more absurd, than the Scrum Bolo Chihuahua.

Until I get back to my apartment building, and past Doorman Dave, and upstairs to my front door.

Where I find something more absurd.

CHAPTER
23
Toucan or Not Toucan, That Is the Question

My mother wakes me up the next morning waving what I hope is a white flag. A white flag that will be followed by "I give up! I give up! I never should have dated that hairy-chested Drill-A-Kid! And I never should have made you spend the night at a house with hard pillows!"

But it is not a white flag.

It is a yellow sheet of paper.

"Why is your principal sending me this, Timmy? Why? What now?"

But I don't know what it is. So she holds it up in front of me.

```
          NOTICE OF ADMINISTRATION MEETING
     WITH YOUR CHILD,  ___Timothy Failure___


Dear Parent(s),


This is to inform you that on Monday, April

3, Principal Alexander Scrimshaw would like

to remove your (son) daughter from (his) her

regularly scheduled class from 1:00 to 1:30

p.m. in order to discuss:

_____ _____ _BEHAVIORAL ISSUES_____.


If this meets with your approval, please

initial below.


_____
```

"Well, obviously he has an agenda," I answer. "Who's to say with that despot?"

"Timmy, this is serious. *They will kick you out of school,*" she says with the monotone delivery she saves for just these occasions.

"I have no idea what he wants," I answer.

But of course I do.

The Beast talked. Yapped. Sang like a canary.

"Listen," I continue. "For all I know, Scrimshaw wants to talk about his *own* behavioral issues. The man is a moral degenerate. And while we're talking about behavioral issues, since when is it okay to kiss a man who looks more like Sasquatch than a—"

I am cut off by the bark of an animal. But it is not Sasquatch.

"What in Sherlock's name was *that*?" I ask.

A dachshund peeks out from behind my door.

"A sausage dog?!" I cry.

"Relax, Timmy. It's only Lucifer. It's Rick's dog. He asked if I could watch him while he attends a coaches' clinic. I didn't think you'd mind."

"What are you running here—*a zoo*?? First the cat. Now *this*?"

"It's just for a few nights."

"A few nights? How many times do I have to tell you? We have a polar bear! He could crush those two with a twitch of his paw."

But I know that's not true.

If anything, the cat and dog will team up to steal Total's wallet.

"Enough, Timmy. Go to school tomorrow and find out what Mr. Scrimshaw wants. But I swear, if you did something else wrong—"

She stops herself and takes a breath.

"Breakfast is ready," she says. "Get up and get dressed."

"Are there any other animals I need to be aware of before I make my way to the kitchen?"

My mother stares at me. And walks out of the room.

"Maybe a lemur in the laundry room?" I call after her. "A gibbon in the garden?"

She doesn't reply.

"A toucan in the tub?"

CHAPTER
24
Hello, Mother, Hello, Father, That Chihuahua Ate Another

I am in the office of Alexander Scrimshaw.

And it is as dry and confetti-less as ever.

STILL NO CONFETTI

"Care to tell me what happened?" he asks.

"I deny everything she said!" I declare.

"Who?"

"Her."

"Who's her?"

"What?" I ask.

"I said—Who is *her*?"

I quickly realize that I have said too much. So I deftly cover my tracks.

"Forgive me, sir. I am still suffering the ill effects of a grievous head injury I sustained at the hands of a beastly sports nut. Ignore my gibberish."

"No, no. Please continue," he says. "I assume eventually you'll come to the part where you tell me why you destroyed Scutaro's costume."

I am caught off guard.

"I . . . what, now?"

"You know," he adds. "Where you ripped the antenna off his head."

"Antenna?" I ask, dumbfounded. "*That's* why I'm here? For that thing?"

THAT
THING

"Ahh, yes. *Now* he remembers. Glad you're feeling better. But too bad Mr. Holmes isn't. He sat right here in that chair you're in now and cried his eyes out. Said you ripped apart his costume. *Maliciously*."

"It was just a—"

"Probation!" he barks. "Remember that word? Remember the little speech I gave you? Or did your head injury erase that also?"

My left eye twitches. Then my right.

"Nervous?" he asks. "Well, you should be. Because this is your last warning, Mr. Failure. If I hear anything else bad about you from Mr. Holmes or anyone else in the school, you're gone. Finished. Do you understand?"

I nod. He glares.

"And I don't think your mother would like that."

I get up and open the door of his office.

"Oh, and one more little matter, Timmy," he adds. "There's been a rumor about a stolen nature report floating around school. A report that supposedly got a very high grade many years ago. Now, I *know* you don't have anything to do with that. Even you're not that crazy. But in case you know anyone who *is* that crazy, you might want to tell them that we've decided to change some of the requirements for the project this semester. You know, so old answers can't be repeated."

He pauses.

"If you know what I mean."

He smiles. It is oily. Like the greased wheels of belching machinery.

"So, Mr. Failure, the majority of whatever you collect—you know, leaves, bugs, what have you—will have to come from an overnight field trip the class will be taking."

"An overnight trip?" I ask, the words leaving my mouth involuntarily.

"Oh, yes," he answers. "To a very unique little ecosystem."

I summon the courage to ask one more question.

"So where are we going?"

Scrimshaw smiles.

"A place called Camp Monkeychuck."

CHAPTER
25
Good-bye and Good Luck

"Timmy, it's one night. You'll be fine," says my mom. "Now do you have everything?"

"You were a good mother," I answer. "I suppose we should shake hands."

"Stop being so dramatic, Timmy. Now do you have the flashlight that Dave gave you?"

Dave being Doorman Dave.

"Yes," I answer. "Although his note showed a profound ignorance of my profession."

"Well, it was very thoughtful of him. I told him how you were feeling about the trip, and he wanted to give you something to make you feel better."

"You shared my business with the *doorman*?"

"He cares about you."

"Mother, he's a paid employee of the building. Please. Show some discretion. Did you share my business with the sports nut as well?"

"Timmy, stop."

"Did *he* give you a gift for me also? Perhaps some baseballs you could throw at my head?"

The intercom beeps. "There's a Ms. Tookus down here for you," says Doorman Dave.

"Thanks, Dave," says my mother into the intercom.

My mother looks back at me.

"Well, Timmy, I guess Rollo and his mom are here to pick you up."

She holds out her open arms.

"Are you gonna hug me?"

I hesitate.

"What?" she asks. "Not discreet enough for you?"

I jump into her arms, almost knocking her over with the weight of my backpack.

"Take care of my polar bear," I tell her. "He gets very, very lonely."

"I will, sweetie."

"And make sure you feed him. If you don't, he'll eat Señor Burrito."

Breakfast

"I know."

"And maybe that stupid sausage dog, too."

LUNCH

"I know, baby. I know."

"Oh, and I left a last will and testament. You know, in case. I don't really have much stuff to give away. So I sort of just filled it in with whatever. It's on the fridge."

"Okay, Timmy, okay," she says, smiling. "I'm sure you'll be fine. I love you."

I don't say anything back. Detectives are rarely comfortable expressing feelings.

So I just turn and run for the elevator.

Not quite sure if she will read what I left on the refrigerator.

But hoping she does.

CHAPTER
26
Misguided Angel

The badness begins on the bus ride.

"Did you find it?" asks Angel de Manzanas
Naranjas, leaning urgently over my seat.

"If you recall," I answer, "I am no longer your detective."

"You are now."

"What are you talking about?"

"Corrina Corrina quit. That little flake."

WORTHLESS AS EVER

"She dropped your case?"

"Yup."

"Why?"

"Dunno," Angel answers. "Don't care."

I ponder what this might mean. What scam she is running now.

I lower my voice. "Did you not hear what Scrimshaw said about—"

"It's a lie," Angel whispers back. "The Miracle report is as valuable as ever."

"But Scrimshaw said we have to collect most of our stuff from here at this—"

"Horse puckey," he barks, cutting me off.

"Birds are birds. Bugs are bugs. The fact is they know the Miracle report is out there. And they don't want us using it. So they're just trying to intimidate us."

My detective mind is aflame.

Is it possible that the Beast has found the Miracle report already? Could she have turned it in to Scrimshaw? Maybe *that's* how the unprincipled principal knows about it.

I turn to Angel.

"My rate is twenty dollars a day. Plus expenses."

Angel leans closer, the rough stubble of his cheek brushing mine.

"You'll work for free, or else."

I remain calm.

"I'm the highest-profile person in this school," I warn him. "You won't get away with it."

"I don't care," he says. "I'll beat you up anyway."

It is a good argument. Filled with logic and foresight.

"You have a deal," I say.

The bus pulls off the highway into a dirt parking lot, at the edge of which is a small, run-down diner. An unlit neon sign reads, LIZ'S LUNCH COUNTER.

"We're stopping here for lunch," says the bus driver. "So we're gonna go down the aisle and get each of your sandwich and drink ord—"

His voice is drowned out by the guttural roar of a dozen motorcycles.

The bikes veer around the rear of our school bus and into the diner's parking lot, causing a wave of yellow dust to envelop the bus.

When it clears, we see a slew of enormous motorcycles parked in haphazard fashion across the lot, their shiny chrome reflecting the bright sun. And dismounting from each is a three-hundred-pound hairy behemoth, covered in skulls and horns and tattoos.

Modern-day Vikings.

And they are ready to pillage.

The kids on the bus each struggle for a better glimpse. And are soon stuck to the glass like crushed flies on a windshield.

CARVERETTE ELEMENTARY SCHOOL

I nudge my way toward an open window. "Flo!" I yell.

One of the bikers turns around and walks slowly toward the bus.

"Timmy?" answers the monstrous biker.

It is Flo, my librarian. And he is happy to see me.

FLO
the
LIBRARIAN

"What are you doing here?" he asks.

The other students stare motionless.

"Oh, this?" I answer, pointing back over my shoulder. "Stupid school trip. You know how it is."

"Interesting," he says. "And you're stopping at Liz's for lunch?"

"I guess," I answer.

"Good choice," he answers. "Try the beet-root salad. It's why we come here."

"I'm a red-meat eater myself," I answer, scanning the wide-eyed faces of the kids encircling me. "But between you and me," I add, lowering my voice, "the whole thing's a huge waste of time. Big distraction from my detective business. I just want to get back home, if you know what I mean."

Flo nods.

"Hang on a second," he says. "I've got something for you."

He walks back toward his bike and removes something from the back compartment. The kids on the bus strain to get a better view.

"It's probably a knife," whispers one kid.

"Or a bat," buzzes another.

"Here," he says, handing me a worn paperback book. "It's called *The Odyssey*. All about a poor guy trying to get back home. Good read."

I take the book from Flo.

"Interesting," I tell him. "I'll give it a look."

Flo nods and lumbers back toward the

diner. The wooden diner door slams behind him.

The silence of the bus is broken by a frightened voice from just over my shoulder.

"I'll pay whatever you want," murmurs Angel.

CHAPTER
27
I'm Being Followed by a Rude Shadow

Once at Camp Monkeychuck, we are assigned cabins and a bunkmate.

My fortunes in a downward spiral, I am paired with none other than Scutaro Holmes.

A.k.a. Monkeyboy.

"Half monkey. Half boy. He's the official mascot of Camp Monkeychuck," says Scutaro. "And I get to wear the costume because everyone voted for me in the camp survey!"

The camp survey. A form we were asked to fill out on the bus. My responses to which were apparently in the minority.

Official Camp Monkeychuck
Survey Form

Greetings, children! And welcome to Camp Monkeychuck! We hope you enjoy your stay here and have a rewarding experience! Please take a moment to answer a few questions.

1) What are you looking forward to the most at Camp Monkeychuck?

GOING HOME.

2) What arts and crafts project would you like to make at Camp Monkeychuck?

A KEY THAT WOULD ALLOW ME TO STEAL THE BUS AND DRIVE BACK HOME.

3) Who is most deserving of wearing the coveted Monkeyboy costume?

ANYONE BUT SCUTARO. UNLESS HE CAN HELP ME STEAL A BUS.

"So how much stuff have you collected here so far?" asks Monkeyboy. "I already have twenty-three new bugs."

On the far side of the cabin, Rollo stops unpacking. He walks over to Monkeyboy.

"How'd you do that?" he asks Scutaro. "I thought we weren't supposed to start collecting until the nature walk this afternoon."

"I got 'em from the grove," he answers.

"You went into the redwood grove?" asks a wide-eyed Rollo. "They told us *not* to."

"They told *you* not to," answers Monkeyboy. "Class presidents get special privileges."

"That can't be!" cries Rollo, his head shaking from side to side. "You'll get an A and ruin the curve for the rest of us!"

"Breathe," I tell Rollo.

"I could end up with a B plus!" yells Rollo.

"Now look what you've done," I say to Monkeyboy.

"We can't all get A's," he replies.

"Auuuugggghhh," cries Rollo, his head accelerating.

"You know, Rollo," adds Monkeyboy, "if you're really that worried, maybe you ought to get hold of the Miracle report. I hear that's what a lot of people are doing. I bet your pal Timmy knows all about it."

I suddenly have an urge to throw Monkeyboy up a tree. But visions of Scrimshaw dance in my head.

So I gather my composure.

And stare down the Monkeyboy.

"For your information, Scutaro *Holmes*, I know nothing about the Miracle report."

"Really?" asks Scutaro. "'Cos Corrina Corrina says you've done pretty much no work on the nature project. That tells me you're counting on cheating. In fact, I think you might have been the one who stole that report."

"Lies! Falsehoods! Calumny!" I chant.

"Timmy would never have stolen that," interjects Rollo.

"Oh, yeah?" continues Scutaro.

"He doesn't care enough about grades," adds Rollo.

"Well, don't take my word for it, Rollo. Corrina Corrina thinks he stole it, too."

The cabin door swings open.

And a long shadow cast by the afternoon sun creeps up the cabin wall.

Followed by a female voice.

"Shut up, Scutaro."

CHAPTER 28

Into the Pit from Whence She Came

The Beast asks if we can talk and leads me away from the cabins.

I scan the bushes for assassins.

"We can talk in here," she says, stepping down gingerly into the camp's tug-of-war pit, now devoid of water.

Wary, I stop at the edge of the pit.

"C'mon," she says. "This camp is so filled with annoying blabbermouths. I think we're safe from them in here."

I check the horizon for bulldozers. It would be just like her to try to bury me alive.

She sees me hesitate on the edge.

"No one's followed us," she says. "If that's what you're worried about."

I climb down cautiously into the hole and stand on the damp, boggy ground. But I keep my distance from the Beast.

"Have you ever seen so many people paranoid about grades?" she says, opening the conversation with small talk. "All this stuff about stolen reports, cheating. I hate it."

I stare at the high dirt walls of the tug-of-war pit. It is a symbolic neutral ground between two opposing forces, each dedicated to the other's destruction.

She tilts her head to one side.

"Okay, first off," she confesses, "I *did* make the mistake of telling Scutaro you hadn't done much work on the project. That was stupid. I didn't realize what a big mouth he had. But I never told him you stole the Miracle report. Really."

I remain silent.

She sighs.

"Okay, Timmy, listen. I understand why you're mad at me."

I ponder the reasons.

REASONS I'M MAD AT THE BEAST

- ✓ Evil
- ✓ Corrupt
- ✓ Vicious
- ✓ Depraved
- ✓ Vicious
- ✓ Sinister
- ✓ Foul
- ✓ Heinous
- ✓ Hideous
- ✓ Beastly
- ✓ Malevolent
- ✓ Vile
- ✓ Loathsome
- ✓ Repugnant
- ✓ Repulsive
- ✓ Revolting
- ✓ Bad breath
- ✓ Dresses funny

"You're mad because I agreed to take Angel's case," she says. "I get it. But the only reason I agreed to do it was to get the Miracle report myself."

"HA!" I cry, breaking my silence. "You fraud!"

She laughs.

"It wasn't so I could cheat, Timmy. I wanted it so I could get rid of it. Make sure that nobody else could use it. I swear. On the detective's code."

"Mendacity!" I shout.

"Mendacity?" she repeats. "You think I'm lying?" She begins to walk toward me.

"That's close enough," I warn.

She stops.

"Timmy, you can believe all this or not. But it's true. It's why I took the case. And it's why I *dropped* the case when Scrimshaw announced that most of the nature samples would have to be collected from here, Camp Monkeychuck. I figured the Miracle report no longer mattered at that point."

She puts her hands on her hips.

"Are you not going to talk at all?" she asks.

I squint and rub my chin. "Words are cheap," I answer.

She walks toward me again.

I hold up my hand for her to halt. She does not.

I step back but slam into the wall of the pit.

"Listen to me, Timmy," she says, her foul breath just inches from my nose. "I want to get the best grade I can on this nature report. And that means we have to work together. Now, I didn't pick you to be my partner. And you didn't pick me. But it's the situation we were given. And we have to make the best of it."

I look to flee, but my feet are glued like suction cups to the marshy soil.

"Now, I don't know what all that stuff was about in my dad's bank," she continues. "Or why you'd want a bunch of old bank records. But right now, I don't care. I just want to get this project done. And the next twenty-four hours are the time we have to do it. I'm willing to work with you. *Are you willing to work with me?*"

Before I can answer, I hear a loud muddy *SPLAT* and am speckled with flying mud.

"Rollo Tookus, what are you doing?" I ask. He stares up at us.

"I'm so sorry," he says. "I followed you because I heard you talk about grades and the Miracle report, and I just sort of slipped and fell in and—"

"Has everyone in this camp lost their mind?" shouts Corrina Corrina.

"Ohhhh, I'm sorry! I'm sorry!" cries Rollo.

I wipe the splattered mud from my face. "Since when do you care about the Miracle report?" I ask Rollo. "And since when is it okay to eavesdrop on a professional detective's conversation?"

"I know. I just . . . I just don't want anybody to cheat. I mean, I don't know if the Miracle report is really helpful or not, but if it will affect the curve and—"

He stops.

"You don't have any idea who took it, do you?" he asks.

Corrina Corrina stares at me. I stare back.

"If you don't know, maybe I can help," adds Rollo, shrugging his fleshy shoulders. "You know, find out what you know. Work with you—"

"Work with her," I say, pointing at Corrina Corrina. "*Somebody* has to."

CHAPTER 29

Nature Walk This Way

The afternoon nature walk is a futile exercise in futility.

Because I can't collect enough of anything to catch up with the others.

So I use the time to find the one thing that can save me.

The Miracle report.

"Benedici, I want to talk to you," I whisper to Nunzio Benedici, last in a line of kids walking past a row of oak trees.

"What about?" he asks, shoving something up his nose.

"What was that?" I ask.

"What was what?" he says.

"The item you just shoved up your nose."

"Acorn," he says. "I have twenty-two of them in there."

I lean over and peer up his nostrils. "How do I know that's not the Miracle report in there?"

He pauses.

"I don't think that would fit up my nose."

I quickly make a note in my detective log.

"Is everything okay?" asks Nunzio.

"Maybe," I answer. "But keep your nose clean, Benedici."

"That may be hard," he answers.

I try to grill more witnesses. But they are too obsessed with finding leaves and bugs.

So I condense my interrogation to an easy-to-fill-out form.

I am soon second-guessed by amateurs.

"Couldn't people just lie?" asks one camper.

"*Of course* they could lie," I answer. "Which is why I follow it up with a second questionnaire."

I am tallying the "No's" when I run into the broad back of Rollo Tookus.

"What are you stopping here for?" I bark.

"Look," he says, pointing to the right.

I look to the right and see a gravel path.

A path that leads to a redwood grove.

"Keep walking," I tell Rollo.

"That's the grove," he says.

"I know what it is, Rollo. Now keep going. We're falling behind the group."

Rollo stares at the redwood trees.

"I have to get an A," he says. "Scutaro went in there. He's gonna beat me."

"Get a hold of yourself, Rollo. You're delirious. You said yourself that the grove is filled with deadly dachshunds or chihuahuas or whatever they are."

"It's probably not true," he says.

"You said campers get *eaten* in there, Rollo."

"I know what I said, Timmy. But Scutaro went in there. *He* survived."

"Scutaro did what?" asks a deep voice from behind us.

It is one of our camp leaders.

And he looks familiar.

"Did one of you little punks go into the grove?" he asks, pointing toward the redwoods.

"You're Crispin Flavius," I say.

"*Mr.* Flavius. And who—"

He stares at me wide-eyed.

"Oh, God," he says.

"You dated my mom," I tell him. "Remember, I crashed your Cadillac into a house?"

MEMORY LANE

But Crispin Flavius doesn't answer.

And doesn't look like he needs a reminder.

"I think he remembers you," says Rollo.

CHAPTER
30
Monkeychuck Prison Blues

Each camper at Camp Monkeychuck is given one five-minute phone call before they return to their cabins for the night.

So I call my mother.

"Well, Timmy, how is it?" she asks.

"Like prison," I answer. "But less fun."

"Oh, it can't be that bad."

"It is. And your boyfriend is here."

"Rick?" she asks. "Mr. Drillashick?"

"The one before."

"Crispin?"

"Yes, him. And unlike your current boyfriend, he hasn't thrown anything at me."

I hear my mother sigh.

"Speaking of which," I continue, "how's our lawsuit coming against Coach Drill-A-Kid? Is your army of lawyers taking his every last chest hair?"

"Timmy, we're not suing your baseball coach. And let's not waste this call talking about the lawyers in my office. They're not worth it."

"What happened?"

"Nothing. They're just rude."

"I noticed that. Perhaps as their head, you should outlaw them. Or at least restrict their comings and goings."

"Can we talk about something else?" she asks.

"Yes," I say. "Did I get any business correspondence? I don't want to miss any cheques."

"You didn't get any cheques. But you did get a postcard from Molly Moskins."

"Molly Moskins? What does that unrepentant criminal want now?"

She reads me the postcard.

"*'Hola, Timmy. Te extraño! Como esta mi gato?'*"

"What the . . . ?" I exclaim. "It must be code."

"Timmy, it's Spanish."

"She's probably threatening our lives. Or wants us to smuggle spoons."

"I doubt it."

"Give it to Total and tell him to use our code-breaking software. By the way," I add, "did you feed him?"

"No, Timmy, I haven't fed Total."

"What do you mean you haven't fed him?"

"Timmy, I just got home from work."

"Mother, do you have any idea how homesick that bear has been lately? If you don't feed him, he'll abandon all hope and flee for the Arctic!"

"Okay, okay. I'll feed him."

"Good," I answer. "Where is he?"

"Uh, I don't know," she says.

"Mother, he's a fifteen-hundred-pound polar bear! How can you not see him? Is he *gone*? *Is my polar bear gone?*"

The other campers in the phone line stare at me.

"Timmy, calm down," says my mother. "I'm sure he's . . . Well, look. . . . There he is now."

"What's he doing?"

"He's on the . . . balcony. Yep, there he is. Watching the sunset."

"You're making that up! Total never watches the sunset! Sunsets depress him! *Where is my polar bear?*"

"Your phone time's up," says one of the campers in line behind me.

"Timmy," I can hear my mother say, "everything is going to be—"

"The rule is that you get five minutes!" yells another camper from behind me.

"Will you please hang on?!" I shout back at the campers. "I have to—"

The line suddenly goes dead.

"Rules are rules," says Monkeyboy.

CHAPTER 31

Long as I Can See the Flashlight

As the sun sets, I lie in my bed and draw.

TRAPPED IN A FOREIGN LAND OUR HERO FACES AN **UNCERTAIN** FUTURE....

FILLED WITH BEASTS...

CHIHUAHUAS!

RRR-

MONKEYS!

UNPRINCIPLED PRINCIPALS!

But the night fights back.

"Hey, turn off the stupid flashlight," yells someone.

"We want to go to sleep," shouts someone else.

"What do you think you're doing?" asks another.

And from the bunk above me:

"Draw your lame comic later!" adds the Monkeyboy.

So I turn off the flashlight.

And put down my pen.

And brave the night.

CHAPTER
32
Bathroom Break

Beset on all sides by light-haters, I take my flashlight and sit in the gravel outside the cabin.

It is a long night. But I am alert.

To every sound.

And every movement.

Of even God's tiniest creatures.

As well as his round ones.

"Never sneak up on a detective," I warn him.

"Sorry. Can't sleep," Rollo whispers.

"Me either," I answer.

"I think I worry too much," he says. "What about you?"

"I just have a large brain," I answer. "And sometimes it keeps me up."

Rollo nods.

"I wish this whole thing were over," he says. "Camp. The nature report. The—"

"Listen, Rollo," I cut him off. "I don't want to hear about your twenty-three bugs and your thirty-three leaves, and how many more Scutaro has than you, and how it almost made you run into that stupid forest. The whole thing is ridiculous. And I don't care."

Rollo says nothing.

"'Cos if you think *you* have problems," I add, "*I* have a partner I can't work with. And *no* bugs and *no* leaves. And a case I haven't solved. And a report I cannot find. So if you don't mind, I'd like to just get through this night and not worry about *you* and all your dumb grades."

"SHUT UP OUT THERE!" I hear from inside the cabin.

I glare at Rollo.

"And now look," I whisper. "You've gone and woken everybody up."

Rollo starts to walk away from our cabin. "Follow me," he says. "I know somewhere we can talk. Somewhere where there's light."

I follow him past a row of cabins toward the boys' bathroom. It is a bathroom I have avoided ever since discovering that none of the stalls has a door.

"See? They keep the light on in there," Rollo says, pointing toward the bathroom. "It won't be as dark."

I follow Rollo inside. It takes a moment for my eyes to adjust to the light.

"So it's not really the grade stuff I'm worried about," he says, leaning against a dirty sink.

It is then that I notice he has one hand behind his back.

"It *is* the grade stuff you're worried about," I reply. "Which is why you have your hand behind your back. You're crossing your fingers."

"No, I'm not," mumbles Rollo.

"You are."

"I'm *not.*"

"Show me."

"No."

"Show me your hand, Rollo Tookus!"

He slowly pulls his hand out from behind his back.

And true to his word, his fingers are not crossed.

But they are holding this.

"The Miracle report," I mutter.

He nods.

"That can't be," I answer.

"It is," he says, dropping his head. "I stole it."

I stare at him. Silent.

"This is so bad," he says, his head beginning to shake. "Sooooo bad."

"Start talking, Rollo Tookus."

He takes a deep breath. His head decelerates.

"It was a few weeks ago after class," he begins. "Just a normal weekday afternoon.

But one on which I volunteered to clean the storage cupboard in Mr. Jenkins's classroom."

"You are quite the kisser of butts," I remind him.

He ignores my commentary.

"So I was dusting, you know, stacking school supplies, that sort of stuff. And all of a sudden, I saw this one piece of paper sort of sticking out from the bottom of a pile. And something on it caught my eye."

"Was it a cupcake?" I ask, aware of his penchant for fatty snacks.

"No. It wasn't a cupcake. It was the grade written on it. In red pen. It just said, 'A+++++.' An A with five plusses. *Five.* I've never even *seen* a grade that high. And there was no one around, so, naturally, I had to look at it. So I pulled it out of the stack. Very slowly. And I see it's the front page of a report. A *nature report*."

Rollo wipes a bead of sweat from his broad, round forehead.

"So you just took it?" I ask.

"No. No. Well, not exactly. I mean, I heard a sound. Someone walking back toward the classroom. So I panicked. Shoved the report under my shirt."

"Who was it?"

"Mr. Jenkins!"

"Did he notice?"

"No. I don't think so. But I knew he would if I stuck around. So after he said hello and started walking toward his desk, I just took off. Ran right out of the classroom."

"You *fled*?"

"I was petrified. So I ran for the playground. The far end. Out by the tetherball courts. It was as far from the school as I could get. I didn't know what else to do."

"You fool," I tell him. "In that kind of situation, you *always* eat the evidence. *Always*. It's detective code."

EVIDENCE

CHOMP
CHOMP
CHOMP
CHOMP

"Yeah, well, I'm not a detective, Timmy. And I was scared. And then I got even more scared."

"Why?"

"Because all of a sudden, I saw Dondi walking toward me."

"The yard lady?"

"Yeah, so I knew I had to dump it. And *fast*. And that's when I saw the big trash can by the tetherball courts. So I walked over and just casually threw it in there. Then I tried to cover it up with some juice boxes and lunch bags."

"Did Dondi see you do it?"

"No. But I wasn't able to cover it very well."

Rollo hears a noise from outside the camp bathroom. He walks outside but finds no one.

"So what happened?" I ask when he steps back inside.

"I don't know," he says. "But the next thing I knew, the Miracle report was all anyone was talking about."

"So Dondi stole it out of the trash!" I declare, my detective instinct keen.

"No, Timmy, no. It wasn't the yard lady. But it was somebody. And pretty soon all the cheaters in the school had passed it around. And then—well, then it got worse."

"What happened?"

"*Scrimshaw* found out about it! I don't know how. But he found out."

"Scrimshaw stole it!" I declare. "That crooked rapscallion!"

"No, no, Timmy. Scrimshaw didn't steal it. But when I found out he knew about it, I freaked out. Because I *knew* he would find my fingerprints on it. *Knew* he'd kick me out of school. And *knew* that for the rest of my life I would never be able to get a job and would probably be forced to sell oranges by the side of the highway."

"All logical deductions," I tell Rollo. "But with your head being so round, perhaps there would be some marketing possibilities."

"Regardless," he answers, "the point is that once Scrimshaw found out about the stolen report, I knew I had to get it back in my hands and somehow return it to Mr. Jenkins's cupboard."

"Fine," I answer. "But how'd you get it back?"

"Well, that was the easy part," Rollo answers. "One of those cheaters left it sitting on top of his backpack during lunch hour. Right out in the open. So I just grabbed it. And I haven't let go of it since."

"Meaning that you thought it would be a good idea to bring contraband like that to a *school* camp?" I ask, shaking my head.

"What else could I do?" he answers. "I figured they'd search my school locker for sure. So I didn't want to leave it there. And I was afraid to leave it at home while I was at camp. My mother would find it. She's very nosy."

"So why didn't you just throw the stupid thing away?"

"Because I felt so guilty! I had *stolen* it! I *had* to put it back. Had to undo what I did. I just haven't found the chance. Not with everyone looking for it and talking about it and—oh, God, I feel so guilty. What am I gonna do?"

He covers his eyes with his hands.

I stare at the "A+++++" on the cover and ask the obvious question.

"Did you look through it?"

"Oh, no," he says. "*Never*. I swear. Never even opened it. I just couldn't do it. The only thing I saw was the grade and that it was written by someone named Tracy Miracle."

I nod, unable to take my gaze off the report.

"Well, there are a lot of people who *do* want to look through it, Rollo Tookus. A lot of people who *need* to look through it."

I raise my gaze back up to my frightened friend.

"It is the stuff that dreams are made of, Rollo."

Rollo slumps down to the damp tiled floor.

"I know, Timmy. Believe me, I *know*," he mutters.

I see tears welling up in the corners of his eyes.

"I want to get a good grade on that nature report more than anything I've ever wanted in my life," he says, trying to steady his trembling lower lip.

He pauses.

"And it's still possible if . . . if—"

"We glance through it quickly?" I offer.

"No," he says, clutching the report to his chest.

"Then what?" I ask. "And it better be good. Because right now it's everything I can do to not grab that report from you and flee like a hungry rabbit."

Rollo looks up at me.

"It's possible if we go into the redwood grove," he says.

I spring forward and seize him by the front of his Stanfurd shirt.

The Miracle report drops from his hand.

"Rollo Tookus," I shout. *"You are not going into the redwood grove!"*

But my voice is too loud. And I do not hear the approach of feet in the gravel outside the bathroom.

And I do not see Angel de Manzanas Naranjas until he is standing in the bathroom, rubbing his eyes.

"Out of my way," he mumbles. "Gotta use the john."

Rollo's eyes dart toward the fallen report. I glance at Rollo and whip my head back toward Angel.

Whose tired eyes are suddenly wide open.

We all freeze.

And all dive for the report.

But Rollo and I are too slow. And we hit the cold tiled floor as both Angel and the Miracle report fly out the door.

"Angel!" I shout, leaping up after him. But by the time I get outside, he has disappeared into the dark night.

So I dart back inside the bathroom.

"Did you see which way he went?" I ask Rollo.

But he doesn't answer.

Because he isn't there.

CHAPTER
33

Over the River and Through the Woods To the Round-Headed Kid We Go

I burst from the bathroom, flashlight in hand.

"Rollo!" I shout.

But he doesn't answer, and my flashlight goes out.

And I smash into the front door of the girls' cabin.

"What was that?" yells one girl.

"Is it a bear?" screams another.

"Stupid battery!" I grumble, shaking the flashlight.

From inside the cabin, I hear the sound of campers leaping from their beds.

I drop the flashlight and feel my way along the outside of the cabin until I am around the side, where I know the gravel pathway extends in a straight line past the long row of cabins.

And I take off into the darkness, following the sound of Rollo's heavy feet upon the gravel.

KSSH KSSH KSSH KSSH KSSH

"Stop running, Rollo!" I shout. "Stop running right now."

But he doesn't.

And I follow the sound of his footsteps through the swing set, where he hits a swing and sets the rusty chains in motion.

SQUEAK SQUEAK SQUEAK SQUEAK

I dodge the flying swing and turn right along the bank of the stream, where I hear Rollo's large feet clomp over the wooden footbridge.

ka-THUD ka-THUD ka-THUD ka-THUD

I follow him past the camp leaders' cabin, where a porch light goes on, and a tall man rushes out onto the porch.

"Kid! Kid!" he shouts. *"What in God's name are you doing!? It's the middle of the gosh darn night!"*

I stop.

"Oh, hi, Crispin. It's me, Timmy."

Crispin steps back inside the cabin and locks the door.

And turns off the porch light.

I turn around and listen for Rollo and can still hear him running.

So I follow.

Past the arts and crafts cabin.

Around the supply shed.

Through the fire-pit sand.

Over the asphalt parking lot.

Until I am tired and lost.

And surrounded by redwoods.

Where I can hear Rollo breathing.

And by the dim light of the half-moon, I see the heaving visage of Rollo Tookus, lying flat on his back on the forest floor, trying desperately to catch his breath.

"What the heck do you think you're doing?" I shout.

"It's . . . the . . . forest. . . . Had . . . to . . . come. . . . Get . . . good . . . grade . . . on—"

"WE'RE IN THE REDWOOD GROVE!" I scream. "Do you know what that means?! *WE'RE GONNA GET EATEN BY*—"

"You didn't have to follow me!" he shouts back. "Didn't you see where you were running?"

"Of course I saw!" I answer. "But I ran in anyway! That's what detectives *do* in the face of danger! *It's detective code!*"

My voice is cut off by the crack of a twig.

That neither of us stepped on.

And I suddenly realize that I am face-to-face with my inevitable end.

Death at the hands of the Scrum Bolo Chihuahua.

Who in the moonlight looks an awful lot like this:

"What are YOU doing here?" I shout.

"I followed you," she answers.

And smiles.

"Detective code."

CHAPTER
34
The Grand Duel

"I don't understand anything you do," I say, sitting by the campfire my enemy has just made.

"Just be glad I remembered to bring matches," Corrina Corrina answers. "I figured you two were running into the forest."

She surveys the tall trees encircling us like an impenetrable curtain.

"But now I don't know *where* we are," she adds. "Did you have to run so far?"

"Blame Rollo," I answer. "It's all his fault. And how'd you even know we were up?"

"You smashed into my cabin door. It woke up everyone. Plus, I was pretty much awake anyway."

FAULT OF THE DEAD FLASHLIGHT, NOT ME

"What were you doing awake?" I ask.

"I don't sleep well," she answers. "I never have."

I watch as the glow of the campfire illuminates the edge of Corrina Corrina's profile.

"Why don't you sleep well?" I ask her.

"The night," she answers. "It kind of scares me."

She looks back at me.

"Does it ever scare you?"

"No," I respond. "Nothing scares me."

She nods.

"Must be nice," she says. "I'd give anything to be able to sleep like normal people."

As she says it, she glances at Rollo, who is fast asleep by the campfire, snoring loudly.

"Non-detective brain," I say, pointing at Rollo. "Simple and carefree."

Corrina Corrina holds the palms of her hands toward the fire.

"He worries so much about grades," she

says, glancing back at Rollo. "That's how I knew he would come to the redwood grove. He needed to compete against Scutaro."

"HA!" I retort.

"What?" she asks.

"Like you're not part of that? You'll do *anything* to get good grades."

"No, I won't."

"Yeah, right," I answer. "It's how you compete. It's how you compete in *everything*."

THE BACK OF
HER BASEBALL
CARD,
FOR HANDY
REFERENCE

Height: EVIL

Weight: EVIL

Hobbies: EVIL

Occupation: Evil

"Is that how you see me?" she asks. "That's funny. Because that's not how I see you."

"How do you see me?"

"Honestly?" she asks. "Like you-won't-get-your-feelings-hurt kind of honest?"

"Yes," I answer, puffing out my chest and jutting out my chin.

I prepare for a barrage of defamatory insults aimed at me, my agency, and my global reputation.

"I see you as lonely," she says.

"HA!" I blurt out, exhaling loudly. "*Lonely?* That's a laugh."

"Hmm," she says. "Well, maybe I don't know you very well. But I'm always seeing you eating by yourself at lunch and so I just thought—"

"By *myself*?" I ask, incredulous. "For your information, I spend most of my lunch hour with my business partner, discussing agency business."

I clear my throat.

"Perhaps *your* agency would be better if you'd do the same."

Corrina shrugs. "I don't have a business partner," she says. "It's just me."

"Yeah, well, you hardly need one," I answer, unmoved. "Not with all that high-tech detective gear you use as a . . ."

I pause.

"What?" she asks.

"A *crutch*," I finish.

"Crutch?" She laughs. "Timmy, I barely have anything."

"Pshaw!" I answer, in disbelief.

Rollo's snoring builds to a crescendo. I roll him over with my feet to make him stop.

"It's the truth," she continues. "I have some binoculars. A fingerprinting kit. And what else . . . ? Oh, a magnifying glass. But that's about it. To tell you the truth, I'd much rather have a business partner."

She smiles.

"How do you get one of those?" she asks.

"My business partner is a close personal friend," I answer in a matter-of-fact fashion. "And he's quite large and intimidating. And that's all I'm going to say."

The wood in the fire crackles as one of the logs splits.

"I live alone with my father," she says.

I say nothing.

"But he's barely home," she adds.

"Hmmph," I answer.

"Is that what it's like with your parents?" she asks.

"I only have a mother," I reply. "And she's home *too* much."

She laughs.

And slides closer to me.

"That's close enough," I caution.

"Okay," she says.

And looks over at me.

"Do you know what an emperor penguin is?" she asks.

"Who doesn't?" I answer.

EMPEROR
PENGUIN

"They live in Antarctica," she says.

"Of course they live in Antarctica," I reply. "I know a great deal about the Arctic poles."

"Oh," she says. "Well, then maybe you already know what makes them so unique."

"Go on," I offer. "We're both lost in the woods. We have nothing else to do."

"Okay," she says. "Well, with emperor penguins, both the mom and dad penguin go to the coldest part of Antarctica every year to have their egg, right?"

"The *mom* lays the egg, not the dad," I remind her. "And that's hardly unique."

"Yeah," she says. "I know. The mom lays

the egg. But you're right—that's not what makes them so special."

"So what is it?" I ask. "What makes them special?"

"Well, after she lays the egg, the mom penguin leaves," she says. "Goes to the sea to feed. And she's gone the entire winter."

"The whole thing?"

"Pretty much."

"And what about the dad?" I ask.

"That's what's so interesting. The dad penguin never leaves the egg," she says. "Not for a minute."

I watch as another log cracks in two, sending embers up into the night air.

"So why are you telling me this?" I ask.

"Because when I'm home, and I'm alone, I have an imaginary friend," she says, lowering her voice. "And his name is Frederick."

"Frederick?" I ask.

"An emperor penguin," she answers.

And pauses.

"And he never leaves my side."

The pyramid of logs in the fire collapses,

splintering into smoldering chunks. We watch as the individual coals burn.

"I have a polar bear," I volunteer, staring at the collapsed fire. "That's . . . my business partner."

"Imaginary?" she asks.

"Anything *but* imaginary," I answer. "He's big and fierce and protects me from everything."

She moves closer to me.

"I bet he's the greatest polar bear in the world," she says.

"He is," I answer. "He really is."

"You know, polar bears and emperor penguins are from opposite poles," she says.

"I know," I answer.

"Do you think ours would get along?"

She puts her arm around my waist. It's cold, so I don't resist.

"I don't know," I answer. "Total's fierce."

"Is that his name? Total?"

"Yes. Total."

"Is Total always fierce?"

I stare at her eyes, no longer black, but now twinkling with the reflected firelight.

"Maybe not always," I answer.

She smiles. And tilts her face toward mine.

And I kiss her.

Because my lips are cold, too.

And as if I've angered the gods, the forest erupts.

In a cacophony of terrifying sound.

Of giant trees being shoved aside like matchsticks. And timber breaking. And branches being crushed.

"The Scrum Bolo Chihuahua!!!" I yell, waking Rollo. *"He's gonna EAT us! We're all gonna DIE!"*

Rollo jumps to his feet, as does Corrina Corrina. And the three of us stand frozen in fear, staring into the foreboding grove.

And as I peer into the darkness, I see the hulking frame of a massive creature part the curtain of redwood branches and leap toward us with enormous strides, landing with a thud at the foot of the campfire.

"It's him! It's him!" I shout to Corrina Corrina. "My business partner! Here to save us! Follow me!"

I trail after my bear as he crashes through the forest, following the path Rollo and I used to enter.

And as we exit the forest, Rollo passes me.

And I pause there, on the border between the trees and the clearing, between the dark of the forest and the moonlight of the meadow, to make sure my polar opposite is safe and still following.

And she is.

CHAPTER 35

The Fugitive

The Miracle report was not done making miraculous appearances.

As it did in the office of Alexander Scrimshaw, shortly after we returned from camp.

"I found it sitting on top of Angel's backpack," sneers Scrimshaw. "And he says he got it from you, Rollo."

Yes, the very same Angel de Manzanas Naranjas that left the stolen Miracle report sitting on his backpack the first time left it sitting on his backpack a second time.

And when Scrimshaw nabbed him, he ratted out Rollo.

"He had it with him in the camp bathroom," says Angel. "So I just grabbed it to return it to you, Principal Scrimshaw."

Interestingly, Angel's account made no mention of me. For he still feared *my* angel.

FLO
the
LIBRARIAN

"The only reason I'm not suspending both of you *right now*," Scrimshaw lectures, "is that neither of you appears to have made use of this stolen paper."

Yes, after all that struggle, neither of them actually used the famed Miracle report. Rollo on principle. And Angel because Scrimshaw grabbed it before he could.

Which was a fateful development.

For as it turned out, Tracy Miracle was a student from many years back who had received special permission from the school to collect her nature specimens *not* from local habitats, but from her family's safari in Africa. Meaning that her report was filled with a whole bunch of bugs found mostly over there, like the foam grasshopper, the gladiator bug, and my favorite, the African dung beetle.

In fact, of all the people who allegedly saw the Miracle report, only one was foolish enough to actually use what was in it in his *own* nature report.

And he was sitting in Scrimshaw's office, too.

SCUTARO
HOLMES

Stanfurd

It's funny how small he looks when he's not dressed like a monkey or a bug. And he won't be for a while now, because he's been stripped of his mascot costume, his school clubs, and his class presidency, becoming the first elected official in the history of Carverette Elementary School to be impeached and thrown out of office. All dire consequences, but not as dire as the consequences Rollo had dreamed up for himself when called into Scrimshaw's office.

"I'll be kicked out of school! I'll be kicked out of my house! I'll be kicked out of the country!"

None of which happened.

Thanks to his best friend's detective skills.

"We meet again!" I declare as I swing open the door of Scrimshaw's office.

Scrimshaw stands. "What are you doing in here?" he snarls.

"Saving an innocent man," I announce.

"Marilyn," he says into his speakerphone, "get Mr. Failure out of my office right now."

"Your secretary isn't here," I inform him. "She's on a break. Besides, I have all the information you need concerning the Miracle report."

Scrimshaw rubs his eyes and collapses back into his chair.

"It *better* be good," he says.

"It's better than good. It's brilliant," I declare modestly.

I point to Rollo.

"Rollo Tookus had nothing to do with the theft of the Miracle report. Neither did Angel."

I look over at Scutaro.

"Neither did the bug there, but you should probably kick him out of school anyway."

"Enough," Scrimshaw says through clenched teeth. "Tell me whatever information you have right now."

"Fine," I answer. "No one who stole the Miracle report would be dumb enough to *hang on to* it like Rollo did. I mean, sure, Rollo can be stupid, but not *that* stupid."

Rollo frowns.

"It's a compliment," I assure Rollo, and then continue.

"A person would only carry around contraband if they were given it by someone else. Someone else who *had* stolen it, but who had got cold feet and didn't have the guts to return it to Mr. Jenkins's cupboard. So they needed someone else to do it."

"I have no idea what you're talking about," says Scrimshaw. "And I'm about to kick you out of this office."

"Wait. Don't," I plead. "Because I'm about to get to the good part."

"Hurry up," he says.

"Okay, okay," I say. "So if you were a student here who had stolen the Miracle report, and had then got very scared that your theft would be discovered, what would you do?"

Everyone stares at me.

"I keep forgetting that none of you are detectives."

"Get to your point!" Scrimshaw stands and barks.

"Fine, fine," I say. "You'd hand it to trust-worthy Rollo to return. And . . ."

"And what??" asks Scrimshaw.

"You'd flee the country!"

"You'd what?!" Scrimshaw shouts. "What does that have to do with anything?"

"Don't you get it?" I exclaim. "*Molly Moskins stole the Miracle report!* It's why she fled to Peru! She's a fugitive from justice!"

I see Scrimshaw circle around his desk toward me.

"Wait! Wait! I have proof of her criminal-ity!" I announce, holding out the postcard she sent me. "Look! She threatens me in her own handwriting! And she asks me to smuggle spoons!"

But Scrimshaw keeps coming.

"This just says she misses you," mutters Rollo, staring at the postcard. "And then she asks about her cat."

But I don't have time to listen.

For I must flee Scrimshaw's office.

But as I do, I pause in the doorway to cele-brate my triumphant detective skills.

"Confetti," I shout over my shoulder to Scrimshaw as I run. "This place needs it."

CHAPTER 36

If You Build It, Timmy Will Leave

But there was no celebrating in the Tookus household.

For Rollo got his first B+.

And in the end, it wasn't his involvement with the Miracle report that did him in. It was his partnership with Nunzio.

But that was a lot better grade than Angel got. He never bothered to collect *anything* and will most likely be repeating our grade for the third time.

And as for me?

Well, there's the great irony.

It turns out that while I was busy solving the world's highest-profile case, Corrina Corrina was out grabbing every leaf, bug, stick, fruit, and feather that has ever fallen, walked, or wafted onto the ground of Camp Monkeychuck.

And for reasons I can't fully explain, she shared all the credit with me.

And it wasn't a lie. I *had* saved her life. And you need to be alive to get a good grade.

My mother was thrilled with my grade. Though skeptical might be a better word.

Personally, I thought it was fine. It got Scrimshaw off my back. And it made my life easier. Though I suppose I could have been more gracious around certain people.

And speaking of my mother, she had her own victory.

She finally dropped Drill-A-Kid and began going out with someone she said she had dated before.

Both of whom came to watch my last baseball game.

MOTHER DOORMAN DAVE

Which made me rather proud when the cannonball came my way.

And I did not flee.

PLOP

Though I didn't know what to do with it.
So I laid it down on the field and left.

Triumphant again.

CHAPTER
37

Oh, Wonderful . . . Instead of Ending the Book on *That* Glorious Note, Rollo Tookus Has Now Decided to Spoil the Whole Thing by Bringing Up Some Very Unpleasant Business That Will Do Nothing But Ruin the Book for All of You, So, Please, Let Me Apologize in Advance for This Chapter, Not to Mention the Absurdly Long Title

"You know, I saw you kiss Corrina Corrina," says Rollo Tookus.

"What?" I answer from atop my mother's new Roomba. "You saw nothing of the kind. You were delusional with fear and you passed out."

"Yeah, but then I woke up. And I saw you kiss her. It was gross."

I leap from my Roomba and poke Rollo in the chest.

"*First off*, anything you saw was agency business and, as such, is guarded by the detective code of confidentiality!"

"Yeah, but I'm not a det—"

"*Secondly*, nothing happened."

"But it—"

"*Thirdly*, if something did happen, it was a matter of life or death."

"Kissing is a matter of—?"

I run to my room and grab the note I had saved from the forest.

"*Read it!*" I say, thrusting the note in front of his nose.

"What does it mean?" Rollo asks.

"What do you mean, 'What does it mean?' It's the only way to save yourself from the Scrum Bolo Chihuahua."

"Oh, yeah," says Rollo. "I saw you write a note in your detective log while you were sitting there."

"Absurd!" I retort. "This was given to me by another camper!"

"But it's in your handwriting."

"Amateur!" I shout. "You know nothing about handwriting analysis. And I certainly didn't invite you over to be insulted."

"All right, all right, fine. So why *did* you invite me over?"

"To help me hang up my agency's new banner."

"That's what that is?" he asks. "That's huge. How were you able to buy that?"

"I was awarded a large sum of money from an entrepreneurs' fund. They have great respect for my business instincts. So I spent all their money on a sign."

"You spent all your money on a Total Failure, Inc. sign?"

"It's *TFI*. But no. We've rebranded ourselves yet again. Now we're just 'FI.' It stands for 'Failure, Incorporated.'"

"What happened to Total?"

"He's been granted a temporary leave of absence. With pay, of course."

"What for?"

"My mother's substandard care left him

traumatized. So I'm letting him spend a few months recuperating on my bed."

"Does he like that?"

"He loves it. The lazy beast. I even painted one of the walls for him."

FOR TOTAL

by Timmy

RICE KRISPIES TREATS

"So no more work for him?"

"Not for now. His last official task was to get our new sign made. Now help me hang it from the balcony."

We each grab an end and carry the sign outside.

Once on the balcony, we hold on to one end and let the large canvas unfurl.

"People of the world, behold," I shout as it unrolls, "the international headquarters of FI!"

"*If?*" asks Rollo. "If what?"

"If you'll excuse me," I answer, "I have a polar bear to fire."

STEPHAN PASTIS is the creator of the *New York Times* bestselling Timmy Failure series, the first of which was a 2014 BookTrust Best Book Awards winner, a runner-up in the 2014 Sainsbury's Children's Book Awards and listed as one of 100 Children's Modern Classics by *The Sunday Times*. He is also the creator of *Pearls Before Swine*, an acclaimed comic strip that appears in more than seven hundred newspapers and boasts a devoted following. Stephan lives in northern California, USA.

Read on for a sneak peek
at the next book in the
Timmy Failure series

A Shocking Prologue That If All Goes Right Will Make You Want to Read the Rest of This Book

We're all in trouble when we can't tell the good guys from the bad.

But tell that to the photographers that surround the entrance to the hotel.

And tell it to the crowd of onlookers who want a glimpse.

And tell it to the police who try in vain to clear a path.

For the bad guy.

Who at precisely 9:07 p.m. is escorted out of the revolving glass doors of the hotel to an explosion of flashbulbs.

The lingering effect of which produces a bright ball of light in the center of his gaze.

Making it impossible to see the faces of the surging crowd.

As a cop shoves a photographer. And someone screams. And a woman faints.

And the bad guy is pushed through the throng.

His hands now cuffed.

His shoes quite scuffed.

A world gone mad.

The good now bad.

CHAPTER 1

Let the Fireworks Begin

It is a fireworks show like no other.

"Sit back, Timmy," says my mom.

"But I want to watch."

"There's nothing to watch," she says.

And as she says that, another large bug explodes across the windshield of our car.

"Ooooh, that was a big one," I say. "Very colorful, too."

"Timmy, we have hundreds of miles left on this drive," says my mother. "Now sit back or I'm stopping the car."

I sit back. But am hit in the arm by my polar bear.

"Ow!" I yell.

"What now?" asks my mom.

"My polar bear hit me."

It's true. He does it every time he sees a Volkswagen.

"That does it," says my mom, who before I know it is pulling our rental car into the parking lot of an E-Z Daze Motel.

"You can't stop here," I tell my mother. "We're in the middle of nowhere."

But she doesn't answer. She just gets out of the car and says something to Doorman Dave, who has pulled his car in next to ours.

Doorman Dave is my mother's boyfriend. He's called Doorman Dave because he used to be the doorman in our apartment building. But now he got a job far away, so we're using my precious spring break to help him move.

And it is tragic beyond comprehension.

Tragic because I have stared at nothing but cornfields for hundreds of miles.

OH, LOOK...MORE CORN.

Tragic because it has all been to the tune of my mother's favorite country musician, Slim Chitlins.

And tragic because of the effect it is having on a boy a world away.

A boy named Yergi Plimkin.

CHAPTER 2

Meet Yergi Plimkin

Yergi Ismavitch Plimkin is from somewhere that is not here.

And he has no books.

A fact discovered by my peace-loving, world-saving classmate Toody Tululu when she saw Yergi's large face in a newspaper ad.

TOODY TULULU

NEWSPAPER AD

YERGI PLIMKIN'S FAMILY HAS NO BOOKS FOR YERGI TO READ...

CAN YOU HELP?

So Toody organized a charity, Yergi Ismavitch Plimkin, You Are Poor. While the name wasn't flattering, the acronym was catchy:

And so YIP YAP held bake sales and car washes and bike races until it had raised enough money to buy poor Yergi Plimkin some books.

That amount being:

"Zero dollars and twelve cents," read YIP YAP's vice president, Nunzio Benedici.

"What?" exclaimed a shocked Toody Tululu at the monthly meeting of YIP YAP. "Read that again, Madam Vice President."

"I'm a boy," replied Nunzio. "I can't be a Madam."

"Read it again, anyway."

So Nunzio read the amount again.

"That can't be," said Toody Tululu. "We had one hundred and twenty dollars at our last meeting and we haven't spent a dime."

"I don't know what to tell you," said Nunzio, looking at the ledger. "It's not there."

And with that, peace-loving Toody made a brief, yet cogent, statement.

SOMEONE WILL DIE FOR THIS!!!!!

You'll have to read *Timmy Failure: Sanitized for Your Protection* to find out what happens next...

TAKE A BREAK
BETWEEN CASES

Even the head of a global detective agency needs to relax.
You can't fail to have fun at **www.timmyfailure.com**

Watch videos

Free activities

Play games

TOTAL MUST BE FREE

MIND GAMES WITH ROLLO

Learn how to draw your favourite characters!